The Book of Dares for Lost Friends

Jane Kelley

SQUARE
FISH

Feiwel and Friends
New York

SQUARE
FISH

An Imprint of Macmillan
175 Fifth Avenue
New York, NY 10010
mackids.com

Our books may be purchased in bulk for promotional, educational,
or business use. Please contact your local bookseller or the
Macmillan Corporate and Premium Sales Department
at (800) 221-7945 ext. 5442 or by e-mail at
MacmillanSpecialMarkets@macmillan.com.

Library of Congress Cataloging-in-Publication Data

Kelley, Jane (Jane Alice),
The book of dares for lost friends / Jane Kelley.
pages cm
Summary: "New York City middle-schooler Val teams up with a
strange boy who lives in an even stranger bookshop to save her best friend
who has lost her way in this story about universal friendship" — Provided
by publisher.
ISBN 978-1-250-07983-1 (paperback)   ISBN 978-1-250-08014-1 (ebook)
[1. Friendship—Fiction.   2. Magic—Fiction.   3. New York (N.Y.)—
Fiction.]   I. Title.
PZ7.K28168Bo 2015
[Fic]—dc23
2014049060

Originally published in the United States by Feiwel and Friends
First Square Fish Edition: 2016
Book designed by Ashley Halsey
Square Fish logo designed by Filomena Tuosto

1 3 5 7 9 10 8 6 4 2

AR: 8.0 / LEXILE: 500L

For Alex, Kira, and Sofia

One

A sleek, black cat walked along the sidewalk. She held her tail high. A shopkeeper shouted at her. Three little children called, "Oooh, kitty." She didn't even look in their direction. She paused briefly to let a yelping dog lunge at her. She always knew the exact limit of their leashes—and that she would never ever have to wear one. Then she flicked her tail and continued on.

Her name was Mau. She belonged to no one. No cats ever really do. They accept our offerings of food and devotion. They allow us to admire their beauty and copy their images for our amusement. We can only pretend to comprehend what goes on inside their minds. But we do know this. They are always thinking something intense and complex and extraordinary.

Mau moved purposefully, looking neither right nor left. She knew exactly where she was going. She didn't hurry; she had no need. Unlike the people and the cars rushing past her, she was supremely confident that the world would wait for her.

After crossing a narrow street and then a much busier and wider avenue, she stood on the sidewalk next to a dark gray stone wall. It was nearly ten times her height. She crouched down, twitched her tail several times, and then leapt to the top of the wall. She stood there for a moment. Was she admiring her own prowess? Or was she staring into what lay beyond?

And what was there? Trees, grass, playgrounds, baseball fields, hot dog vendors, benches, ponds, statues—in other words, all the ingredients of a park.

Central Park was beloved by New Yorkers for providing a respite of green from the dense concrete canyons. Much of the park had been sculpted to amuse the citizens. But there were still places that had not been touched. Tangled forests where wild animals lived. Murky ponds. And gigantic rocks that could have been the tops of mountains if they weren't buried in the ground.

Mau leapt off the wall and entered the dark, untamed heart of the city.

Was she hunting mice? Sparrows? Squirrels? Pigeons? She had feasted on them all. She preferred to find her own food, unless someone made an offering of a can of tuna. Putting the best parts of a great fish inside a small tin was mankind's greatest accomplishment. Or so it seemed to Mau.

She passed underneath several thickets of bushes and emerged in the shadow of great gray boulders flecked with shiny bits of quartz.

Two girls sprawled on top of the larger of the two rocks, surrounded by what was left of their lunches, their backpacks, and a bright yellow bag.

"Mau!" they cried.

Mau did them the honor of ignoring them. She sat at the base of the rock and licked her paw. When she first encountered the girls several years ago, she had avoided them completely. They didn't have any food she liked to eat. The things they called "goldfish" were actually small orange crackers. The other items were purposeless sweets; Mau didn't understand why humans enjoyed them so much.

"Hello, Mau. We hoped we'd see you." The girl called Val jumped down from the rock. She never sat still. She was always climbing or kicking a black-and-white ball that was too large to interest Mau.

But the other girl, the one called Lanora, was different. Mau spent a lot of time secretly observing her. Lanora wasn't a cat. She had no tail under her brightly colored skirt. And yet there was something about Lanora that Mau found to be familiar. Perhaps it was the intensity with which Lanora did absolutely nothing.

Mau walked through some bushes and reappeared on top of the rock, next to Lanora.

"Tomorrow is a very important day. There are very few times in our lives when we have the chance to begin again," Lanora said.

Val kicked the ball. It bounced off the base of the rock and returned so she could kick it again. "Whatever you wear will be fine."

"You don't have to think about it. You'll just wear a soccer shirt."

Mau sat on the rock about two feet from the edge of Lanora's skirt.

"And you are always comfortable in your own skin." Lanora smiled at Mau and held out her hand.

Mau sniffed the fingers. She considered whether or not she wanted to be petted at that moment. She bowed her head and accepted a small scratch behind her ears. Then, because Lanora seemed agitated, Mau allowed her to slide her hand along Mau's sleek, black fur. Once, twice, three times—but no more. As it was, a great deal of bathing would be required to set things right.

"You fit your own skin, too," Val said.

Lanora shook her head. "I might be more like a snake. Or a hermit crab."

"Or a butterfly?" Val said.

Lanora opened the yellow bag. She held up a ring attached to a small, lilac-colored butterfly. Its antennae were threads. Its wings were plush fabric. Mau batted at it with her paw.

Val climbed up on the rock and took an orange butterfly out of the bag. She grabbed her backpack and examined the objects that dangled from a ring at its side. "We got puppies in third grade because we were sure we would get real ones that year."

"Instead my parents got divorced!" Lanora said with forced enthusiasm.

"Trolls in fourth grade," Val said.

"Because our teacher looked like one."

"Flashlights in fifth grade because we could finally walk all by ourselves to each other's apartment buildings."

"Except after dark."

"And butterflies this year because . . . how did you explain it?" Val said.

"It's time to stop crawling around on a leaf and fly."

Val clipped her orange butterfly to the ring with all the other dangles.

Lanora stared at hers as it lay limply on the palm of her hand. "Except these won't ever fly."

Val shook her backpack. The objects rattled but didn't fall. "Now I'm ready to start middle school."

Lanora said nothing.

Mau kept her eyes on Lanora's hand as she clenched the lilac butterfly in her fist.

Val picked up the trash from their lunch and stuffed everything in her backpack. "I'd better go home. Mom says if we want cookies, I have to help her. Don't worry, she won't let me mess them up too badly."

"I'm not worried," Lanora said.

"Are you coming, too?" Val said.

"I think I'll stay a little longer," Lanora said.

"Okay. See you tomorrow," Val said.

The two friends hugged. "'Bye, Mau." Val ran off through the park, kicking the ball as she went.

And so only Mau saw what Lanora did with the lilac butterfly.

New York City was on a grid. Lanora could remember the exact moment she figured this out. The boxes were rectangles instead of squares, but the numbered streets proceeded in order north and south. This was incredibly comforting, especially after her father moved out three years ago. She still knew where she was at all times. And even more importantly she knew where she was going.

After she left the park, she walked three blocks to what would be her new school. Middle School 10. The doors were locked. The brick walls refused to reveal secrets. That was okay. Lanora had already spent a lot of time studying a map of the new school. She wouldn't wander the halls with a lost look on her face. She would stride confidently from room to room, and sit in the seat she had chosen for herself—close to the windows in the third row. From there she could watch the other kids interact. There would be new kids, because M.S. 10 accepted students from several elementary schools. And so Lanora could pick totally new friends.

She continued on toward the apartment building where she lived with her mother. She didn't pass Val's building. If she wanted to walk to school with Val, Lanora would have to go four blocks out of her way. Val hadn't seemed to notice this important fact.

Lanora entered the lobby of her building. She took great care to step on the blue tiles of the floor and never the brown, even though she was a firm believer in making her own luck. There was an elevator, but it was so slow that Lanora always chose the stairs. As she climbed to the third floor, she considered her clothing options. Something fun and frivolous? Something dark and meaningful? Something eye-catching? Something aloof? Who did she want to be? She was troubled by her indecision.

In the past, she had always known what to wear. This was her particular kind of talent. She knew with the certainty of solving math problems what went with what. But she had never been in middle school before. The stakes were higher now.

"Lanora? Is that you?"

Her mother, Emma, was in the kitchen. Lanora came in and gave her a hug.

"Dinner is almost ready. I'm making fish. It's supposed to be brain food. Although why that would be, I have no idea."

"I like fish." Lanora smiled.

"I don't. It's so hard to get rid of the odor. For days after it's gone, you can still smell it."

The phone's sharp jangle pierced the room. Lanora let her mom answer.

"Hello? . . . Oh. It's you."

It was Lanora's father.

"Before you talk to her, I want to ask you. . . . I know you only have a few minutes, but this is important, too. . . . Then why don't you call when you do have time to talk? . . . I can't believe that you never have more than five minutes. . . . Yes, I have timed your conversations. . . . Because I wanted to be able to prove to you that you don't spend nearly enough time on your daughter . . ."

Lanora left the kitchen and went into her bedroom. She shut the door. She opened her window and swung her legs out over the sill so that her feet touched the metal slats of the fire escape. It was a law that each building in New York

City must provide an alternative exit, should disaster strike. There had never been a fire, thank goodness, and yet practically every day Lanora needed to escape.

The space between the apartment buildings was a deep pit. Lanora tried not to think about what was at its bottom. She wasn't afraid of heights; however, she was extremely afraid of falling. And so she clung to the metal bars even as she sat cross-legged on the platform and looked up toward the sky.

Two years ago, a thirty-story building had sprung up in the vacant lot behind them. It cast a permanent shadow across their apartment. Her mom had complained bitterly that the whole world was against her. But Lanora chose to imagine the future when she would be living in its penthouse. One night, while entertaining vivacious people, she would take one of the guests out to her balcony and point down down down.

"That's where I grew up," she would say.

"You sure have come a long way," the guest would say.

"Yes, I have."

But she wasn't there yet. A slight breeze reminded her that where she sat was more space than actual bars. She tightened her grip. Flecks of rust stuck to her sweaty hands. That wasn't reassuring. The air was eating away at the metal. Just like the doubts gnawing at Lanora's mind. She needed to decide what to wear.

Maybe she shouldn't have buried the butterfly dangle after Val left. What if that brought bad luck? But she couldn't just throw it away. And she certainly couldn't walk through the halls of her new middle school with a bunch of junk dangling from the bottom of her backpack. She couldn't even wear a backpack. She wanted to carry something sleek and black. Something that would command respect from everyone who saw it.

Lanora pulled herself up so that she stood on the platform. Her father was always telling her to make the hard choices. He said the difficult things were the only ones worth doing. She couldn't care less if some people didn't understand. She spoke out loud, so that the skyscraper could be her witness. "I have to do what I have to do."

Two

A huge wave pushed Val back against the wall, but she stood her ground. She would not be moved from this spot.

The first day of school was over. All the students surged out of M.S. 10. The eighth graders were impossibly tall. Val saw at least three sixth graders get trampled when they weren't quick enough to get out of the way. Had this happened to Lanora? She wasn't very big. And yet Lanora was fierce. Val decided not to worry. She kept waiting at the place where they had said good-bye that morning. When, for some reason, Lanora had hugged Val more tightly than she ever had in their whole lives, and then run into the building.

They hadn't had any classes together. This bit of bad luck had a logical explanation. The students were grouped according to the foreign language they were studying. Val was taking Spanish. At the last minute, Lanora said she had been told to take French. Val couldn't think of anyone who would dare to tell Lanora anything.

As the last stragglers left the building, a girl read Val's shirt and tossed a soccer ball at her. "Come on, Pelé. We need a forward."

Val hugged the ball for a moment and then tossed it back. "Maybe tomorrow. I'm waiting for my friend."

And she kept waiting until the security guard shut the door.

Val slung her backpack over her shoulder. The dangles bounced against her leg as she walked. She suddenly remembered that when she had seen Lanora that morning, Lanora's dangles weren't hanging from the metal ring at the corner of her backpack.

Maybe the ring had broken. Things broke all the time. But Lanora was usually extremely careful about all her possessions.

At the corner, Val petted a dog until his owner led him across the street. She decided she might as well pick up her little brother from his after-school program.

Drew was six. He had tied his jacket over his shoulder like a cape. "I'm glad you came. I need a staff."

"A what?" Val said.

"For thunderbolts." Drew stared up at his sister as if that were obvious. He led the way to Central Park. He carefully selected a long stick and removed its extraneous branches. He waved it in elaborate figure eights and pointed it at Val. He repeated this three times before Val realized she was supposed to fall down. When she finally crumpled onto the dirt, she died much too quickly, without any groans or moans.

"You are so bad at this. We need Lanora. Where is she?" Drew said.

"I don't know," Val said.

"You go to the same school," Drew said.

"Yes. But it's a big school now. And we don't have any classes together," Val said.

"You have lunch," Drew said.

"I didn't see her. I waited outside, but she must have gone to the cafeteria," Val said.

"Why would she do that?" Drew said.

"I don't know," Val said again.

Drew adjusted his cape and then pointed his staff at his sister. "Call her. The squirrel minions are plotting to overthrow the kingdom."

Val took out her phone and sent a text. COME TO THE PARK TO FIGHT SQUIRREL MINIONS?

The answer came back instantly. BUSY.

It was short. But many texts were short.

"She's busy," Val said.

"How do you know she's busy?"

Val showed him the text. He took the phone and stared at the word for a long time. "How do you know she sent it?"

"It came from her phone. See?" Val pointed to Lanora's name and number.

"Yes, but how do you know that it isn't from the evil Werd?"

"Who?

"The evil Werd has kidnapped Lanora and stolen her phone and sent you a message so you won't come to his secret lair. He especially doesn't want you to bring your brother Drew whose name is his name spelled backwards."

Val laughed.

"You laugh at Werd? You will pay the price for not taking him seriously."

He tackled Val. Soon they were rolling on the ground.

"Stop, stop," Val said.

"Don't you know anything? You can't just tell me to stop. You have to overpower me. Or bribe me."

"I have cookies." Val took out her lunch bag. She had carefully saved the cookies her mom had sent for her and Lanora.

Drew squinted into the bag. "Those aren't cookies. Those are crumbs."

"They are former cookies." She popped a piece in her mouth.

"Don't eat them. They are poisonous to you. Only I have built up an immunity." He took the bag.

"Share, you barbarian." Val tackled him. They rolled over and over, grunting and cursing in Grog.

They stopped when they reached the Bower.

Drew sat up and took Val's phone. He stared at the message for a long time. Then he handed the phone back to his sister. "Ask Lanora again. Tell her we have cookies. She'll do anything for them."

Val sent another text. WANT MOM-MADE COOKIES?

Drew watched the phone intently until a message appeared. He assumed the power of his vision could rearrange the letters to make the meaning that he wanted.

"She's coming, right?" Drew said.

Val sighed and shook her head. She let him read the words. STILL BUSY.

Lanora put her phone decisively down on the table. She wasn't lying. She was busy. She lay back on her bed and stared at the ceiling again. She imagined a slide show of the faces she had seen in school that day. Glasses, pimples, braces, freckles, dimples, smiles, frowns, frizz, buzz cuts, braids. An amazing array of riches to choose from. How would she decide? She eliminated all who looked dazed or confused. The first requirement was that her new friends must be just as determined as she was.

Like Val. There was no stopping Val, if she needed to move a ball across a line drawn in the grass. Lanora looked at her phone where the text remained. She smiled. Squirrel minions had to be Drew's idea.

Should she explain what she was doing to him? Or to Val? How could she say that she had to avoid Val for the time being? But Lanora had to. Val was too comforting. Val was a pair of shoes worn in just right. They were great shoes. Lanora had no intention of throwing them away. She just wanted to be able to wear some new ones, too. Val occupied a space that couldn't be filled by someone else.

Goth, geek, jock, princess, nerd, punk, emo?

Even if Lanora had to sit all alone in the dreaded cafeteria for a few days, she was thrilled to have possibilities.

Candidate 1: A large girl. Dyed-black hair. Wears only one earring and a pop tab on a chain around her neck. Sardonic smile. Plays the electric bass? Or just the ukulele?

Candidate 2: A tall guy. (Yes, why not have a friend who is a guy?) Buzz cut to control his curly red hair. Quiet. Still waters run deep? Or is he too shy?

Candidate 3: A tiny girl. Supreme posture. Her body is

like a marble statue. Walks on her toes because she is a dancer? Or because she is short?

Candidates 4, 5, and 6: Three girls moving as one. Each with sleek blonde hair. Yellow, platinum, ash. (Who knew there were so many shades of blonde?) Gliding along the halls. Everyone watching them. Everyone wanting to walk with them. No one dared.

What was the source of their power? Could Lanora get it for herself? Or would she have to become one of them to find out?

She sat up and stretched. She didn't have to choose today. Rushing such an important decision was not wise. After all, she hadn't exactly chosen Val, either. Somehow or other they had become friends in preschool. Probably because they were the only little girls who had no interest in playing with dolls.

The stakes were much higher now. No matter how hard it was, Lanora vowed to remain silent in her classes. To observe. To be aloof. To be the cat. To watch and wait. To say nothing to anyone.

She stood in front of her mirror and practiced a Mona Lisa smile. She was thinking great thoughts, even if she refused to share any of them.

There was something wrong with her image. She lifted her chin. She tilted her head left and then right. Then she realized what it was.

"You want to do what to your hair?"

"It has to be straight," Lanora told her mom. There was nothing to discuss. Nothing to decide except how this was to be accomplished. "I want to go to a hair salon to have my hair professionally straightened."

"We can't afford luxuries like that. Your school supply list is three pages long," Emma said.

"He sends us money." Lanora knew her father had plenty. She didn't know exactly how he paid her mother for his freedom. She was too young to know the terms of the divorce settlement.

"I have to save that money. I can't trust him. He forgets he even has a daughter."

"He can't. His assistants remind him." Lanora remembered the card she got last year. *Happy Birthday to my darling daughter. From, Miss Campbell.* Lanora and Val had laughed about it—at the time.

"I love your curls." Emma reached toward the auburn waves that framed her daughter's face.

"It's time for a change." Lanora firmly shut the bathroom door. Over the past three years, she had gotten used to doing things for herself.

She washed her hair. She got out the blow-dryer. It was trickier than she expected. She had to point that nozzle like a gun at her head. Her curls kept springing away from the brush. The noise and heat were intense. And yet she was glad for the roaring sound. It helped her ignore her mom's footsteps pacing in the hallway.

Finally Lanora was satisfied with how she looked. She was especially pleased when her mom shrieked. "You don't look like my little girl anymore."

That was precisely the point.

Three

Cats can nap at any time and in any place. Mau's best sleeps, however, occurred inside a shop on the ground floor of a brownstone residence. At the front of the shop, a display window revealed a shelf crowded with objects. A tall, wooden fetish with startling blue eyes. Several small statues of black cats with the bodies of Egyptian women. A brass bowl full of beads. A cracked vase. A rusty knife. The only available space was on top of an open book. Mau had curled in a ball upon a map of Mesopotamia, her tail tucked under her back legs, her paw over her eyes as if to say, Don't bother me, I'm being enlightened.

Perhaps she was. The morning sunshine somehow managed to penetrate the grime on the glass and bless Mau with dancing dust motes.

But the Earth turned. New York City traveled slightly farther from the sun. The dust became invisible once more. Mau sighed, as cats sometimes do. With regret? With contentment? With longing for a different kind of world? Who knows what cats dream.

A man approached the entrance to the shop.

Mau opened one eye.

The sign outside the window began to sway. A painted eye rimmed in thick, black lines seemed to wink.

The man shoved a packet of envelopes through a slot in the rusty iron gate and ran away before the packet hit the floor. *Plop.*

Mau shut her eye. The mail had come.

From the back of the shop, heavy footsteps hurried to the door. The Captain was always eager to see what was in the envelopes. Mau couldn't care less about the pieces of paper. She much preferred the crates that came from far away, some still smelling of the desert.

"What do we have today?" The Captain grunted as he bent over to pick up the letters. "Any checks? Any checks? Bah. Nothing but bills." He tossed the envelopes one at a time into a trash can. Then he stopped and opened a letter.

"What's this?" He read it to himself. He leaned against a stack of crates and then he read it again.

"Someone wants to buy the bowl," he whispered.

Mau sat up.

The Captain carefully folded the letter and slid it back into the envelope. "Boy! Are you here?" he called.

There was no answer.

"Is he here?" the Captain asked Mau.

Mau blinked. Whatever she knew, she wasn't about to say.

"I hope he hasn't gotten in trouble. School started up again. He probably forgot to take that document that says he goes to . . . what did I call it? Oh, yes. The Charter School for the Study of Ancient Antiquities. Boy! Are you here or not?"

When the silence had settled, the Captain took out the letter again.

"I'm going to sell it. Ten thousand dollars is a lot."

Mau narrowed her pupils until they were slits.

"Quit looking at me like that. He could use the money."

Mau twitched her tail back and forth. It rasped across the page of the book.

"What are you doing on that book anyway? You've got your filthy cat hair all over it." The Captain waved the letter at her. "Go on, get down from there. Not everyone is a cat worshiper. How do you get in here anyway?"

Mau's tail knocked over a small statue. The Captain stood it up again.

"I bet I can get more than ten thousand. It's in excellent condition. Considering that it's sixteen hundred years old."

The man and the cat stared at each other. The cat won the contest.

"There aren't that many treasures left in the box. Why shouldn't I sell the bowl? His grandfather is dead."

Mau looked toward the entrance. A moment later, the bolt rasped as it slid back. The hinges creaked. The door opened. A boy's voice said, "Captain?"

The Captain put the letter inside the pocket of his blue coat and carefully fastened as many of the brass buttons as he could. "Shhh," he cautioned Mau.

Mau resumed her nap. No one needed to tell her to be silent.

Four

anora's silence continued all throughout Thursday. Behind the curtain of her sleek hair, she thought great thoughts. She refused to share any of them. Like a cat, she observed everything and said nothing. Not a "thank you" when the girl next to her picked up Lanora's pencil before it could roll completely out of range. Not a "hi" when she encountered someone that she knew. Not an "excuse me" when she stepped on the heel of a boy who wasn't walking as fast as Lanora. Few ever did.

Candidate 2 was disqualified when he wore a shirt branded with the name of a department store. Candidate 3 was disqualified for shrieking when she laughed. Candidate 1, whose name was Helena, was still possible. She hadn't embarrassed herself in math class. Candidates 4, 5, and 6 weren't in any of Lanora's classes, but she had learned that Alicia, Anna, and Ariel were called the A Team—and not just because all their names began with the letter A.

On Friday, Lanora's shirt was red, her apple was golden, and so her book had to be blue. The color wheel would wobble if it didn't balance. She sat at the edge of the third table on the left side of the cafeteria. She was glad this was the last day she would have to eat alone.

"Don't you love those poems? Everybody reads *Wuthering Heights,* but I like Emily's poetry better," Helena said.

Lanora couldn't admit she had chosen the book for its cover. She smiled inscrutably at what she was supposed to have been reading. But she was really studying the group of girls. One had gone to Lanora's elementary school. Lanora had never known what to think of Gillian. But as she stood with these other girls, her clunky boots made sense. Another girl had short black hair with bangs angled severely across her forehead. The last girl had short dreads that almost prevented her from being pretty.

Helena took the book and turned the pages quickly until settling upon a poem. " 'No coward soul is mine/No trembler in the world's storm-troubled sphere/I see Heaven's glories shine/And Faith shines equal arming me from Fear.' "

"What does she mean by 'heaven's glories'?" Gillian said.

"She means what people always mean. Shafts of light piercing the clouds," said the girl with black bangs.

"Don't despise beauty," said the girl with dreads.

"Who cares about that part? I'm more interested in anything that arms you from fear," Helena said.

Lanora wondered what would arm her from fear? She remembered the butterfly dangle she had buried in the park. Was it a paradox that Val still carried hers, when Val had no need of a talisman?

"I'd rather be fearless," said the girl with bangs.

"You are, Tina," Helena said.

Lanora took a tiny bite of her golden apple. She wasn't going to make her choice until Monday. But she liked how bold Helena was. She seemed proud to be intelligent.

When the bell rang, Lanora tossed her apple into the large gray trash barrel and walked along with the girls.

"I think you're in my math class," Helena said.

Lanora shrugged. "If you can call it a class."

"More like an assemblage of primates," Helena said.

"Don't be so insulting to the Bonobos," said the girl with dreads.

"Olivia adores Bonobos," Tina said.

"Just saying the name makes her happy," Gillian said.

"It's a poem all by itself. You try it. Bo-no-bo," Olivia said.

Lanora politely declined. She wasn't quite ready to join in their games—yet.

Then something totally unexpected happened. As they all left the cafeteria, Lanora was separated from their group by a triangle of three other girls with blonde hair as sleek as helmets. Perhaps that was what armed them from fear?

The A Team stared at Lanora. Their mouths smiled, but not their eyes.

"We wondered if you wanted to go shopping," Alicia said.

"We think you might be good at it," Ariel said.

Lanora braced herself for a wicked twist. What were they talking about? Was this an invitation? If so, to what? Shopping seemed far too mundane for them. Skydiving was more like it. Or tightrope walking. Or surfing on top of a subway car. Some feat of daring that would prove their power.

It seemed safest to dislike everything. Lanora tilted her head and let her hair fall in front of her left eye. "I hate shopping. It's boring."

"Not this kind," Anna said over her shoulder as the A Team walked on.

The girls in dark clothes had waited. Lanora was going to the aforementioned math class. She could have walked with Helena and resumed their conversation about shields and Bonobos and the storm-troubled world. Instead Lanora paused for a sip of water. The drinking fountain offered little more than a dribble. But she continued to walk alone for the remainder of the day.

School ended. Students spewed from the building as if from an agitated bottle of seltzer. Lanora lingered inside, where she knew Val wouldn't be. She didn't think Val would like the A Team. It was true that Val had blonde hair like theirs, but that was the only thing they had in common. Luckily the A Team emerged from the girls' bathroom. They barely looked at Lanora. They just assumed she would fall into step with them as they glided out the door and along the sidewalk, on their way to go shopping.

This was New York City. There was no shortage of stores. Monstrous department stores. Trendy boutiques. Exotic emporiums. Each neighborhood had a different delight. SoHo. Fifth Avenue. Even nearby Columbus Avenue had plenty to offer, if they didn't want to take the time to go across town.

Shopping was a fantasy for Lanora. She tried on personas as well as clothes. Sometimes she picked the ugliest thing off the rack and found a way to make it work. She didn't think she would propose that game to the A Team. They were the types who always had their own plan.

They passed the classic jean store, the designer knock-off store, the hat store, the ethnic store—and stopped in front of a grocery store.

Lanora waited. Were they pausing to check their phones? Get out a piece of gum? Adjust the swoop of their hair?

The A Team stared at Lanora. Lanora had never seen such a collection of inscrutable masks. Such narrow noses.

Such delicately arched eyebrows always on the verge of being raised.

They moved a little closer to the grocery store. The door sensed their presence and opened for them.

Why would they want to go shopping here? Lanora tightened her smile to hide the fact that she had no idea what they wanted her to do. As they watched her, waiting, Lanora began to understand. The whole point was that they knew the answers *and* the questions; nobody else did. Lanora was smart, however. She could figure it out. First she had to discover if she was being initiated into their group—or set up for a huge humiliation.

Lanora had seen a lot of other abuse at school. Victims tripped on the stairway. Crammed in a locker. Shoved face-down in a toilet. The members of the A Team were too cold to do anything overtly cruel. They couldn't care less about you. Well, so what? Lanora had endured plenty of indifference from her father.

She briskly entered the grocery store. To browse? No thrill in that. To buy? Obviously not. That left only one possibility. She couldn't even pause to consider what she was doing. Or why she even wanted to be one of them. Her only thought was that this was a game she intended to win.

She had in mind a jar of baby food. Taking it would be her comment on their game. You are babies, she wanted to tell them. She found the shelf lined with little glass containers that had adorable pictures on the labels. Unfortunately the aisle was crowded with moms smiling at their actual babies and boys putting more jars on the shelves. Lanora felt the clock ticking. Like all games, there would be a time limit. She couldn't wait until she could be unobserved. She had to go to Plan B.

She headed for the mounds of colorful fruit in the produce section. She wanted to take an apple. A for apple. A for A Team. The red would have matched her shirt. It would have been perfect.

Then, just at that crucial moment, she saw Val's mom enter the store.

Five

It was Friday. The first week of school was over. Val had learned the shortest distance between her classes, which drinking fountain spouted the highest, which teachers would appreciate a little joke and which were best suffered in silence. Val had joined a soccer team. They ate lunch together near the dog run. Val had no shortage of new friends—including some who liked to get scratched behind the ears. And yet, mysteries remained. Why was there so much homework? Why were some stairways empty and others clogged with kids? And why didn't she ever see Lanora? Was it possible that Lanora had stopped going to school?

After dinner, Val's parents suggested a nighttime walk. Drew immediately put on his cape and grabbed his staff.

He ran down the four flights of stairs and out the door to hide behind the box elder. As Val came outside, he pointed his staff at her. She staggered and fell to the sidewalk.

Drew sighed. "That wasn't the death ray."

"Then what was it?" Val said.

"The transporter. I sent you back in time so you are in elementary school just like me. Ha ha!" He laughed triumphantly and shook his staff in the air.

"Good," Val said.

"You don't mind?" Drew sounded disappointed.

"Nope," Val said.

"Why not? What's wrong with middle school? Is there something I should know?" Drew said.

Val shook her head. She didn't want to talk about how Lanora was acting. She didn't want to get Drew started. "Curiosity killed the cat."

"Really? Curiosity kills cats?" Drew said.

"Of course not," Dad said.

"That's a relief. Because I'm curious about everything. I even want to know the things I don't know I don't know. But I'm especially curious about whether Lanora escaped from the evil Werd."

"What about Lanora?" Mom said.

"Nothing," Val said. When the light changed, she stepped down from the curb. Middle school did have one advantage—she could cross the street by herself. She didn't want to give her mom the chance to ask uncomfortable questions, like why Lanora didn't come over anymore. She used to practically live at their apartment.

"Werd is my diabolical enemy. As you know, his name is my name spelled backwards," Drew said.

"We know," Mom and Dad said.

"Werd kidnapped Lanora on the first day of school and took her to his secret dungeon carved into the bottom of a cliff right next to the ocean. When the waves come crashing in at high tide, you can't get there at all."

"Not at all?" Dad said.

"Except if you study the tidal charts. Which I have done. So I can help Val."

"With algebra?" Val said.

"What's algebra?" Drew said.

Val hid her smile. Oh, to be innocent again.

They had come as far as M.S. 10. Val hardly recognized her school. The dark courtyard was so unlike the chaos of the day, the building seemed to possess a surreal power.

"That evil Werd has cast a spell upon Lanora. That's how he keeps her prisoner."

"What kind of spell?" Mom said.

"A bad one. You see, she *thinks* she is free. She doesn't even know that Werd has cast a spell upon her. But I know. And I will rescue Lanora!"

Drew raised his staff and ran back and forth in front of the building, shouting huzzahs. He dragged the staff along the bars in the fence until it broke and a dog started to bark.

"Time to go." Dad picked up the pieces and used them to trap Drew.

"We can't go yet. I haven't finished saving Lanora," Drew said.

"You can finish saving her at home," Dad said.

"But she isn't at our apartment. She's in the prison," Drew said.

"Then you can save us," Dad said.

And so Drew made a raft out of a sofa cushion and rescued everyone in the family from raging rapids and a large chair-shaped monster named Curiosity. After an hour of this, Val went to do her homework to save herself from being saved again.

"Knock, knock," Mom said, because she was carrying two mugs of tea.

Val's room wasn't much bigger than a closet. In fact, it had been a closet, before Drew was born and needed a room of his own, closer to where their parents slept. Val hung down from the loft bed and opened the door with her toes. She was quite proud of her feet's feat, but it didn't make her happy tonight.

Mom put the mugs on top of the bookcase and climbed up to sit with Val on her bed. She picked up her mug and blew across the steaming liquid. It was still too hot to drink. "I saw Lanora today."

"You did?" Val didn't know what to think about this.

"She was at the grocery store. With three blonde girls." Mom took a noisy sip.

Val moved her mug farther away from a wooden box. Lanora had decorated it with a mosaic of dried beans. Some were missing because she hadn't used enough glue.

"I never saw them at any P.S. 2 events. But that could be because these girls didn't seem to be the participating type." Mom shook her head. "Why would Lanora want to hang around with girls like that?"

Val had to stop this right now. The last thing she wanted was for her mom to get involved in trying to fix something that wasn't even broken. "So what if Lanora made new friends. I made new friends, too."

She hoped her mom wouldn't ask her to name them. Her soccer friends were usually called "dude" or whatever number was on their shirts. Her dog friends were all called Buddy. "It's fine, Mom. Really." She took a sip of tea and burned her tongue.

"I'm sure none of your new friends were doing what those girls were doing."

Mom looked meaningfully at Val until Val had to ask, "What were they doing?"

"I probably shouldn't have gotten involved. But you know me."

Val sighed. She knew her mom all too well. Again and again, she had seen her mom righteously standing up against the cab stopped in the crosswalk, the litterbugs, the people who let pregnant ladies stand on the subway. Righting all the wrongs. In the past, she and Lanora would have laughed about this. But Val didn't know what Lanora thought was funny anymore. "What did you say to her?"

"Nothing. I didn't actually see Lanora do anything. It was the other girls who were eating grapes. Just picking them off the stems and popping them in their mouths. So I said, 'I hope you're going to pay for those.'"

Val groaned.

"Maybe you think, What difference does it make, it's just a few grapes? But I happen to know that poor Mr. Kramer is getting his rent raised again. If everybody ate grapes without paying for them, then how can Mr. Kramer make the rent?"

"What did they say?"

"Nothing. They laughed."

"You should have minded your own business." Val put down her mug with a thump. Didn't her mom understand? Middle school was different. Lanora was different. Maybe even Val was different. She certainly had never felt so hopeless about things before.

Mom patted Val's leg and let her hand linger there. "I'm sorry, sweetie. The next time I see Lanora stealing . . ."

"You said you didn't see her stealing. She was just with some girls who were eating grapes."

"The next time I see Lanora with some girls who are eating stolen grapes, I won't say anything. I'll mind my own business." She sat for a moment. The model of a well-behaved mom. A vapid smile. Sipping tea. Then a little humming. La-di-da.

It would have been comical. Except Val still had to know one last thing. "Did Lanora say anything to you?"

"No. She looked right through me. It was all so strange. Her hair is different. It's so smooth, it made her face seem, well, like a mask."

Then Drew shouted from the living room, "I told you she was under a spell!"

~Six

There was no school on Saturday. No crowded halls. No sitting in classrooms. No histories to learn. Val was so happy. She raced to the practice field in the park and didn't stop running for the next two hours. There were no mysteries in soccer. When she kicked the ball, it shot toward the goal. When she missed the ball, it didn't. She had never appreciated the beauty of this direct correlation before. She didn't have to wonder whether or not she would see Lanora. She wouldn't. That was a huge relief.

But after practice was over, Val did see Lanora with those blonde girls, staring into a store window on Columbus Avenue. Val didn't hesitate; she ran across the street. She had so much to tell Lanora. Val had to apologize that her mom was such a mom about a few grapes, but mainly she wanted to say that she was glad Lanora had new friends. Lanora didn't need to avoid Val because she thought Val might be sad about it.

Val touched Lanora's arm and said, "Hi."

Lanora moved slightly away.

Well, Val was sweaty. The field had been muddy and she had been goalie. That meant she got to dive for the ball. She wiggled her grimy hands. Lanora always used to tease her about being in a laundry detergent commercial.

Only Lanora didn't laugh. She said, "What."

It wasn't the beginning of a conversation or an idea for a new adventure. What if we get empty coffee cans from your mom and tie them to our feet so we can be horses? What are you going to be when you grow up if you have to have glasses and can't be an astronaut? What's the real reason kids have homework? What would you give to get three wishes? What would those wishes be? And don't say to have three more wishes.

Lanora's "what" was the thud after the ball misses the goal and lands out of bounds.

The blondes moved to the next shop window. Lanora traveled with them. None of them picked up their feet as they walked. Val watched. She wanted to see them do something fun or at least interesting. She wouldn't have minded Lanora going off with them if they had been embarking on an expedition to Central Park. Getting lost in the ramble. Laying siege to the castle. Fishing in the lake. They weren't headed out on a grand adventure. They were just gliding along the street. Looking bored.

Val gave up.

By the time the group reached the corner, Val had headed back into the park. And so no one saw Lanora glance over her shoulder and twist her mouth into a very small, apologetic smile.

The Bower hadn't changed. The huge boulders had been there eons before Val and Lanora had claimed the spot. The huge rocks would be there eons after Val and Lanora brought their great-grandchildren to admire the sparkling quartz in the great gray boulders. Val picked up a small stone and tossed it from hand to hand.

Mau came out from the bushes. Val extended her hand, but Mau refused even to sniff it. Once Mau's tongue had brushed against Val's finger—after Val had had tuna for lunch.

Mau paced back and forth along the top of the largest rock.

"If you're looking for Lanora, she's over on Columbus Avenue, busy being bored." Val didn't want to whine, even to Mau. Val despised whiners, even the ones with good reasons.

Val held out her other hand. This time Mau sniffed. Was this the hand that had touched Lanora? Mau looked at Val.

Mau's pupils grew large and then shrank into slits, as if she had seen something she didn't want to see.

"Are you worried about her, too?" Val murmured.

Mau's tail twitched.

"We don't need to be. She made some new friends. At least I think they're friends. What else would they be?"

Mau sniffed the air.

"What do you smell? A squirrel?"

Just then, Mau sprang off the rock. She crouched low and then pounced on something in the bushes. Val braced herself. Usually Mau caught mice. There was one time, however, she had proudly brought Lanora a dead rat.

The branches rustled. Mau seemed to be digging. Val leaned closer to see. Mau made a small sound and emerged triumphantly from the bushes carrying something with wings in her mouth. Dirt clung to the plush fabric, but Val recognized it instantly.

"That's Lanora's butterfly," Val said.

Mau trotted over toward the stone wall that surrounded the perimeter of Central Park. She prepared to jump.

"Give it back!" Val shouted.

Mau easily reached the top and then disappeared down the other side.

Val scrambled up the rough wall. She was much less graceful than the cat. She made it just in time to see Mau, still with the dirty butterfly in her mouth, trotting along the sidewalk, seemingly oblivious to the children who called, "Kitty! Kitty! Kitty!"

Cars and taxis whizzed down Central Park West. Mau used her paw to push the butterfly deeper into her mouth. Then she brazenly darted across the street.

Val watched helplessly on the wrong side of the traffic as Mau headed north, away from the school. She held her tail high as she trotted confidently along. She knew exactly where she was going. She was a cat, after all.

The traffic light changed and Val raced to catch up.

Mau turned the corner. Val followed.

The side street wasn't that far from Val's familiar places, and yet she had never been on it before. This block, like many others, was lined with three-story residences. But these brownstones seemed darker. These trees seemed older. These iron fences seemed distorted. New York City has always been a place where anything was possible. Heroic feats and cruel fates. Royal riches and deep despair. Splendor and suffering. A crazy quilt of buildings. Some new, some old. And some totally beyond the reach of time.

Mau slunk under the gate to one of the buildings.

By the time Val got there, Mau had disappeared. Val climbed up a few steps of a staircase of ornately carved stone, but stopped at the bend that forced anyone who climbed to reconsider. A sign hung from a post in front of the ground-floor window.

ANTIQUITIES FROM THE SHIPWRECK OF TIME

The lettering was faded, but the painted eye below the words seemed to blaze from the wood. The eye was rimmed in black. A long line curled from its corner, like a snake.

Something moved inside the shop. Val peered through the grimy window. It was difficult to see, since the shop was very dark.

Mau was on the other side of the glass. She no longer had the butterfly in her mouth. She sat next to a large open book. Val had never seen one like it before. The page had squiggles where words should have been. Val twisted her head, just in case the writing was upside down. It didn't help. She felt someone staring at her, from the shadows. When she looked up, however, whoever it was had disappeared.

Mau smiled at Val as much as a cat can smile.

"What did you do with Lanora's butterfly?" Val said.

Mau shut her eyes and arranged herself on the book.

So Val pushed open the rusty iron gate and entered the shop. She tried to find the window where Mau was, but she was immediately lost in a maze of wooden crates and shelves burdened with books. They were nothing like the ones for sale at her favorite bookstore. There were no bright colors. No enticing displays. No large cutouts of Eloise or the Cat in the Hat. Just dusty, brown leather bindings. The books seemed so old that this could have been a shop where Shakespeare went in search of something to read. Val opened one volume. It had a map of the world before Columbus made his voyage. Beyond the edge of what had been known, were the words "THERE BE DRAGONS."

It corresponded exactly to the part of the world where she stood at that moment.

"Quit your breathing!" someone shouted.

She shut the book.

A round man pointed his finger at her. His blue jacket couldn't be buttoned. His belly was swathed in a bright red sash. His black beard had one gray streak. "What are you doing in here?"

"Isn't this a store?" Val said.

"There's nothing for you here. Don't waste my time. Go on. Get out." He took the book from her.

"I followed the cat," Val said.

"That dandering fool? That scratching menace?" The man lurched through the shop and put the book in a glass case with several old statues of cat people, a tiny coffin in the shape of a bird, and a dish of glass beads that looked entirely too much like eyes.

"She has something that belongs to a friend of mine," Val said.

He locked the case and shook the key at Val. "I'm not responsible for that cat."

"She's in your store," Val said.

"Stop calling it a store," the man said.

Someone laughed. Val looked behind her, but couldn't see anything except boxes.

The man banged the side of a shelf with his fist. Then he leaned closer to Val. "She thinks she's a Bastet. But she's just an old cat who's running out of lives. And if I catch her clawing one more book, I'll turn her into a mummy and sell her!"

"What's a Bastet?" Val said.

The man pointed to one of the small statues. It had the head of a cat on the body of a woman. It looked Egyptian and old and strange. And yet the cat's head looked exactly like Mau.

"But what is *that*?" Val said.

"I don't have time for your questions. I told you. There's nothing for you here. Now get out." He pointed toward the door. Val walked slowly, looking at the shelves. Everything was so dark and grim, she felt certain she would spot the lilac butterfly, despite its layer of dirt. Once she did see a bit of blue between some crates. But when she bent down to look, whatever it was had disappeared.

"Get out!" the man said again.

She left the store. The iron gate clanged shut. Val came back to peer through the window, wondering what kind of place it was. Mau was still sleeping innocently on top of that illegible book.

"Why did you lead me here?" Val whispered.

"Why did you follow?" someone said.

～Seven～

Val turned around. The sign was swinging wildly. A boy stood next to it. He was about her age, but Val didn't think he went to M.S. 10. He certainly wasn't in any of her classes. He had wild dark hair and a crooked smile. His shirt was an old khaki uniform. Instead of buttons, it was fastened with pieces of shells—or possibly bones. His jeans were very tight. His boots were sky blue, just a little less brilliant than the color of his eyes. She couldn't look into his eyes, so she pointed to the eye on the sign.

"What's that?" Val said.

"A wedjat. The eye of the Egyptian god Horus. The Egyptians didn't think our eyes were just orbs that gather information. They thought our eyes could actually *do* things. Sailors used to paint wedjats on their ships to ensure safe passage up and down the Nile. But I wonder, does this eye protect us or curse us?" He held up his hand. The sign stopped moving.

Val didn't know what to say to that.

"Of course I'm an incorrigible wonderer. For instance, I wonder why the Captain named his shop 'Antiquities from the Shipwreck of Time' and why he even bothers with a sign when no one ever wanders into the shop, except you. But mainly I wonder what your name is."

"Valerie. But people call me Val."

"Yes, yes, I can see that you are Val. For you are brave and strong. You defended yourself against the Captain with great courage and wit."

"He still kicked me out."

"No matter. You held your own better than most."

Was he kidding? Val couldn't tell. "What's your name?"

"Tasman." He pretended to bow. "Perhaps one day people will call me Taz."

"I can call you that."

"No, no. I'm not a Taz yet. But I do believe that in the future, maybe after I have defeated an enemy or performed a perfect dive from the cliffs of the Yucatán, maybe then I could at least be a Taz in training."

Val laughed.

"I'm not very valorous. I am probably de-valorous. No, that would imply that at one time I had valor but lost it. So most likely I am merely un-valorous." He moved closer to the window where the cat still slept. "I wouldn't be talking to you at all except that in a way I feel that Mau has introduced us."

"We call her Mau, too," Val said.

"Why shouldn't you? That's her name."

As if she knew she was being discussed, Mau opened one eye to glance at them. Then she licked her paw with the intense concentration that humans could only aspire to.

"Don't you think it's weird that we would both know that? It's not like she could tell us." Val tried to remember why Lanora had decided that Mau was Mau.

"How do you know she can't? It's true she speaks no English, but she might communicate on a molecular level by causing a fluctuation in the electron magnetic spin, much like what happens in an MRI."

"Why do you talk like that?" Val said.

"I'm a creature from another realm. Like the Captain's other relics, I too have been shipwrecked by time. And so, like many artifacts, I have attributes that are no longer useful. Or admired. Like the deckled edges of the pages of that book."

"The what?"

He sighed. "I will try to control my verbosity." He passed his hand in front of his face, walked backwards and then forwards as if to begin again. "After all, like the torn edges, it's just a way to disguise . . ." His voice trailed away.

"Disguise what?"

"What I really came to tell you is that I will look for your lost item. I'm sure it can't be hard to find. Unless it's an old leather-bound book. We have a surfeit of those, as I'm sure you noticed."

"It's okay. It really doesn't matter."

"Are you saying that the object doesn't matter? Or your attachment to the object? Didn't you say it belongs to your friend?"

Val kicked a rock across the cement yard. Unlike a ball, it didn't return to her. She felt unsettled. Was that because of her mixed-up feelings about Lanora? Or was it because this boy wanted to discuss those mixed-up feelings? "I can always buy another one."

"Buy another one? The significance lies not in the object. If that were true, who would care about bits of old glass? Or scraps of plant fiber pounded into paper? It's the journey of the thing that matters. Its provenance. Where has it come from? Why has it been saved? Where did Mau get it? Why did she bring it here?"

"Why did she?" Although what Val really wanted to know was why Lanora had buried the butterfly in the first place.

"I can answer that last question. So you could meet me, of course," Tasman said.

"Maybe Mau just wanted to take a nap in the window," Val said.

Mau had stopped bathing and was sleeping with her tail across her eyes.

"On that book. That could be significant. Usually she sleeps on that inscribed brick." Tasman pointed to a rust-colored stone covered with tiny marks. The book was indeed much more intriguing.

"What book is it?" Val said.

"It's a book of spells," Tasman said.

"Of what?" Val said.

"Spells."

Val laughed. "That's what I thought you said."

"Why are you laughing? Don't you believe in spells?" He leaned closer to peer into her eyes.

She took a step back. "Do you?"

"I believe in believing. It's a scientific fact that if you believe you'll do well on a math test, then you will do better."

"A scientific fact?"

"Doesn't that sound more convincing than if I said I read it on the Internet? Which I did, by the way. It's as much of a mistake to discount everything one reads there as it is to believe everything."

Val folded her arms. "That still doesn't explain why a cat would bring me here."

Tasman looked at the book again. "Of course these aren't typical spells for altering the weather or getting rid of warts. The actual title is: *The Book of Dares for Lost Friends*."

"What?" Val leaned closer to the window even though she couldn't decipher the strange markings on the page. Then she looked at Tasman. He must have made it up. But how could he have known about Lanora? She turned her back on him and the book. "I don't have a lost friend."

"No, you don't seem the type to misplace anything of value," he said.

"That's right," she said.

"It's a good thing you don't need *The Book of Dares*. But if I find this object that belonged to the careless Lanora, what should I do with it? How can I return it to you?"

"When I'm not at school, I'm usually in Central Park. Playing soccer," Val said.

"You wouldn't consider something a little less dangerous?"

"What's dangerous about that?"

"For you, nothing. You are Val. But for others?" He placed his palm near the wedjat as he went back into the shop.

Eight

The sun crossed the sky. When the wooden sign cast its shadow on *The Book of Dares*, Mau stretched and stood up. Without any farewell, not even a flick of her tail, she snuck out of the Antiquities from the Shipwreck of Time and entered the back alley. She sniffed. The late-afternoon air was full of promise.

Was that dog trapped inside that apartment? Oh, yes. Mau trotted along until she reached the open window. She paused. The beast barked and howled and hurled itself at the screen. Inspiring such emotion in another creature amused Mau for a moment. But a much more urgent question demanded her full attention.

What should she eat? The chances for tuna were good. She hadn't visited her cat ladies in several days. But Mau decided to hunt for her dinner like her ancestors had done. Being in the antiquities shop always reminded her of her illustrious past. In ancient Egypt, cats were worshiped as gods because they killed the mice and rats that would have devoured the Egyptians' golden grain. In New York City, the stores of grain were metaphorical; the mice were real enough. Which variety should Mau choose? Park mice flavored with a hint of wild garlic? Bookstore mice that tasted of leather? Apartment mice that had grown fattest of all on pizza crusts and sweet cereals? Ah, yes. The kind of mice that lived with Lanora.

Mau crept from alley to alley until she reached a tree growing up through a crack in the cement. One of its branches stretched to the fire escape outside of Lanora's window. Mau looked up. The window was dark. The fire escape was empty. Lanora wasn't there.

Mau went past the garbage cans, through a small passageway, and emerged in front of Lanora's building. She hid under some bushes that had been trimmed to look like a green wall. While she waited for Lanora, she caught a mouse and ate it. It tasted of pizza.

Then she heard Lanora coming along the sidewalk. Lanora wasn't talking, but Mau recognized the particular rhythm of her walk.

There were other girls, too. Mau didn't recognize them; none of them were Val. Mau could smell something quite overpowering. A harsh, bad smell, like what humans used to clean themselves instead of their tongues. Then there was another smell, like an animal. But what animal? As the girls came closer, Mau could see that one of them was carrying something about the size of a baby rabbit.

Was it dead? Mau couldn't be certain. It wasn't moving. But they stroked it with as much reverence as if it were alive.

Whatever it was, she knew it was no match for her. She came out from the bushes and sat in the middle of the sidewalk.

The girls shrieked. "Where did that come from?"

Mau smiled. Seeming to appear from nowhere was one of her powers.

Lanora leaned down to hold out her hand to be sniffed.

"Don't go near it. It's a stray," one of the girls said.

Mau moved away from Lanora to sit directly in front of that girl. A stray? She looked up at the girl. How dare you refer to me as a stray.

"Move," the girl said, making feeble gestures with her hand.

Mau wondered how she should torment the girl. Sometimes she liked to rub against the ones who feared her, feigning affection. Other times she would let them see exactly why they should be terrified. What other creature could transform itself from a cuddly thing into a fierce fiend just by puffing up its tail and revealing its claws?

Lanora stood between Mau and the girl, and warned Mau with her eyes.

Mau was confused. Why was Lanora defending this girl?

Why was she with those girls at all? What was that dead animal? Why had Lanora changed her habits? Didn't she appreciate the comfort of continuity in an uncertain world?

Lanora shook her head twice. Mau twitched her tail angrily, but she wouldn't argue with Lanora. Mau arched her back and then walked down the street with her tail held high. She didn't look back at the girls. But she made sure they saw how the tip of her tail curled as if to say, You mean nothing to me.

"Weird," Alicia said.

"Way weird," Anna said.

"Whatever," Ariel said.

Lanora was too agitated to speak. Her toe twitched inside her boot.

Alicia held the small, red leather bag out to Lanora. "Take it."

Lanora frowned. Was this charity? Or a reward for saving her from Mau? "Why?"

"I have plenty," Alicia said.

Charity, then.

"Next time, you can get your own," Alicia said.

"If you don't try for another briefcase," Ariel said.

"Ha ha." But Lanora hadn't wanted just what she could get. A change purse was useless, even if it was made of real leather and had a tiny designer emblem. Lanora longed for a sleek, black leather briefcase with special compartments for important papers, a fountain pen, a phone, and a laptop—the weapons she would wield as she strode into battle.

Alicia gave Lanora the change purse and brought her cheek close to Lanora's cheek. Then Anna and Ariel did the same.

"Ciao," they said.

"Ciao," Lanora said.

When the girls had disappeared around the corner, Lanora looked for Mau. But Mau had gone. Mau wouldn't have let Lanora hold her anyway. Lanora stroked the bag instead. Expensive leather felt so much softer than other kinds. When she got her black briefcase, it would be made from leather like this.

She put the change purse in her book bag and went inside the building. She was in such a hurry that her toe almost touched one of the brown tiles. She managed to avoid that bit of bad luck. She climbed the stairs and let herself into the apartment. She wanted to take the purse to her bedroom, but her mom came over to hug her.

"Where have you been? What is that smell?" Emma said.

"We got sprayed," Lanora said.

"What?" Emma said.

"With perfume in a department store." Lanora laughed.

"What were you doing in a store?"

"Just looking. Don't worry. I didn't spend any money."

"Don't you find it frustrating to look at what you can't buy?"

"Not really. I like to plan what I'm going to do." Lanora carried her book bag into her room. She sat on her bed and took out the change purse.

"Lanora?" Emma called. "Dinner."

"Coming." Lanora stroked the purse one last time and then hid it at the back of her underwear drawer. Then she moved it to the highest shelf, behind the old craft projects. Her mom would never look there.

Emma placed two bowls on the kitchen table.

Lanora vigorously stirred the contents as if that action could change the stew into lobster bisque. Since her mother was watching, she took a big bite.

"Did you have a fun day?" Emma said.

Lanora chewed carefully and finally said, "It was important."

"Important?"

"Yes. It was definitely important."

"I didn't think Val liked shopping," Emma said.

Lanora laughed.

Emma looked hurt because she didn't get the joke. "Well, I didn't."

"She didn't go with me. I went with Alicia, Ariel, and Anna."

"Are they new friends?"

Lanora stared at her spoon. They weren't the type of girls who she would ever share herself with. They were more like business associates. Yes. That's exactly what they were.

"You'll have to have them over sometime," Emma said.

"Sure." Lanora smiled politely, knowing that would never happen.

Nine

On Monday morning, the kids had to wait for the doors of M.S. 10 to open. There were the usual shenanigans, as the gym teacher called them. Somebody's hat was tossed in the air. Somebody's lunch got eaten. The guys lurched around like Frankenstein's monster. The girls squealed, Stop it. The nerds worried that they would be late for their first class. Everybody was packed so tight that Val didn't have to hold her soccer ball. It was wedged among the bodies of her teammates.

Then something parted the crowd of kids. An invisible red carpet created an aisle for a particular group of girls to glide toward the front door. They didn't look happy they were so privileged. Or sorry for those unfortunate beings who got crushed to create this space.

Val watched Lanora pass by. Her face was as expressionless as the other three girls. Like someone really had cast some kind of spell on her.

The A Team reached the front. At that exact moment, as if by personal decree, the doors swung open. They floated on into the school, miles ahead of the pushing and shoving that was the fate of everyone else.

As Val fought her way into the building, she thought how lucky Lanora was to avoid all this. Even if *The Book of Dares* had told Val how to change Lanora back, Val wouldn't have done it. Why would Lanora want to be like everybody else?

It rained during lunch. The heavens opened up. Buckets streamed past the classroom windows. This ruined Val's routine. She couldn't kick the ball with the team. She couldn't go to the bench by the dog run. She had to eat inside. As she bravely marched toward the cafeteria, she passed a classroom with an open door. The teacher's desk was unoccupied, but Val heard people inside.

"It's raining cats and dogs."

"Why cats?"

"Why dogs?"

"Why not rainbow trout?"

Four girls sat cross-legged on the floor. Val barely knew Helena, Olivia, and Tina, but Gillian had gone to her elementary school. This was a much better option than the cafeteria. Val plopped down and said, "Hi."

"Hello, Val," Gillian said.

"Do you eat in here even when it isn't raining?" Val said.

"It's always raining somewhere," Helena said.

"The teacher doesn't mind?" Val said.

"We are a 'club.'" Tina marked the word for scorn with her fingers.

"What kind?" Val said.

"We are the outsiders looking in. We are the voices crying in the wilderness. We are the thoughts which dare not speak their names," Helena said.

"Poetry?" Val said.

"Ding, ding," Tina said.

Val opened her lunch. Today, when she could have shared cookies, there were none. Just a bag of googly eyes.

"Is that candy?" As Olivia leaned forward, her dreads bounced cheerfully around her face.

"It's just my dad." There was no way for Val to explain.

"I remember your dad. He wore a clown nose to parent-teacher conferences," Gillian said.

"Yup," Val said.

"Val and I went to the same elementary school. Val was friends with Lanora," Gillian said.

"The Lanora in my math class?" Helena said.

"The Lanora who joined the A Team?" Tina tilted her head so that the crooked line of her bangs was parallel to the floor.

Val took a bag of grapes out of her lunch bag. Her mom had bought bunches to try to compensate for what those girls had done. Val picked one off the stem and tossed it into her mouth.

"How did that transformation happen?" Gillian said.

"What do you mean, 'transformation'?" The word stuck in Val's mouth. It was too much like something that Tasman would have said.

"Do you need the definition or the reason Gillian has used the word?" Tina said.

"One day she's a gawky girl with too much curly hair," Olivia said.

"And then the next day, she's one of them," Gillian said.

"How did she get chosen to be in their group? Was there an election?" Helena said.

"An application?" Olivia said.

"I missed the deadline," Tina said.

"Wasn't it just yesterday she carried a stuffed animal to school?" Gillian said.

"That was third grade," Val said.

"Third grade!" Tina and Olivia said.

"Tell us more." Helena fingered the pop tab on the chain around her neck.

"It was the middle of winter. I remember snow. Because when I first saw the fur, I thought it was part of her boot." Gillian pointed to her own heavy shoe.

"What kind of animal?" Helena said.

"A dog," Gillian said.

"A duck," Val said.

"That's right. You started bringing the dog," Gillian said.

"Why?" Helena said.

"So people wouldn't tease her," Val said softly.

"That is obvious. I mean, why did Lanora bring the duck?" Helena said.

"She was having a hard time about the divorce," Val said.

"Ah! She wanted to remind herself that however she felt, whatever they said, whatever they didn't say, it would be like water off a duck's back," Helena said.

They looked at the rain lashing the window. They felt glad to be inside protected by the glass.

"I guess it worked. Now look at her," Gillian said.

"A member of the A Team," Tina said.

"Lanora doesn't even start with A," Olivia said.

"It ends with one," Helena said.

"That's not the same thing at all," Gillian said.

"They'll make her change her name," Tina said.

"Change her name?" Val said.

"Anora."

"Aurora."

"Allegra."

"Anagram."

They laughed as they hurled words at each other. And why not? For them, it was a game. They were good at it.

"Angina."

"Aorta."

"Anorexia."

"Algebra."

Val was better at soccer. She stared at the collection of dangles hanging from her backpack. She straightened the orange wings of the butterfly. Had Tasman found its mate? Even if he had, what was she going to do with it? Reattach it to the strap of Lanora's book bag?

No, she decided. She carefully unclipped the rings of her own dangles and put them in the lunch bag with the uneaten grapes.

Ten

On Wednesday, Val saw Lanora in the hallway between 6th and 7th period. On Thursday afternoon, Val saw Lanora getting on a city bus. On Friday, Val saw Lanora coming out of the girls' bathroom. Each time they met, Val greeted Lanora. Lanora didn't respond. Val smiled anyway like everything was normal. After all, this was middle school. Plenty of outrageous things (like stuffing rolls of paper in the toilets) were normal. And plenty of normal things (like greeting someone you knew) were considered to be outrageous.

On Friday afternoon, the kids exploded out of M.S. 10. Everyone was in such a rush to escape; only the poets noticed that something decorated the sidewalk. Val came back across the street to see what they were staring at.

"Look what a child drew on the sidewalk," Olivia said.

"Not a child. Someone too lazy to make proper letters," Tina said.

"A prankster who hopes we'll spend hours deciphering scribble." Gillian pointed to a curlicue with the toe of her heavy boot.

"An egotist who's too self-obsessed to care that no one can read it," Helena said.

"He isn't self-obsessed. I mean, he is. But he does want someone to read it," Val said. Tasman must have copied the beautiful, blue markings from *The Book of Dares*.

"Do you know what it says?" Helena said.

"I don't know what it says, I just know what it means," Val said.

"What does it mean?" Tina said.

It meant Tasman knew where Val went to school. It meant he had been thinking about her. It meant there was something he thought she should do. But she didn't need to. She touched the corner of her backpack. She had gotten rid of her dangles, too.

Just then four pairs of high-heeled boots clicked across the markings. It was the A Team. Lanora passed so close that Val could see one little curl poking out from her sleek hair.

A fifth girl ran up to them. She greeted each member of the A Team by moving her cheek close to theirs. Then they all walked back in the opposite direction. None of them looked at the poets or at Val or at what had been written on the sidewalk.

The poets watched the A Team until they had disappeared around the corner. Then Helena sighed. "I guess they don't like sidewalk art."

The scuffling boots had obliterated the marks.

"Can you remember what was written there?" Gillian asked Val.

Val shook her head vigorously. She was glad she didn't have to worry about the words or Lanora's new friends anymore.

After all, Val had plenty of other things to think about. On Saturday morning, she had to plan which *Three Stooges* episode to watch first. She had to make sure Drew didn't get more than his share of pancakes. She had to decide if she should wear the Pelé shirt or the Hamm. She had to remove her shin guards from Drew's arms and find him some other kind of armor.

At soccer practice, she threw herself into the game. She was unstoppable. She was first at the ball, wherever anybody else kicked it. She always took a shot at the goal, even when other people were more open. She didn't mind who she stepped on as she fought. She just wanted to win win win.

And then she missed a pass. The ball went between her feet and rolled away. She had to run after it. Nothing looked more lame than chasing a runaway ball. Val kept her head down until she reached the wall.

Tasman was there. He was wearing a large hat pulled down over his eyes like a spy in the movies.

Val picked up the ball.

"I left you a message," he said.

"I'm in the middle of practice." She was too busy to talk to strange boys about strange things like undoing strange spells.

"Don't you want to know why I've spent the last forty-five minutes watching you run back and forth in pursuit of a ball, trying to make a goal which doesn't have the meaning that I would prefer for that word?"

"No. It's not any of my business whether Lanora is under a spell or not. She *likes* being part of the A Team. So we don't need to do anything anymore."

"Oh." He looked down at his fist, which was closed around something.

Could it be the butterfly, Val wondered. No, she decided. It was something smaller.

"Come on, Pelé! We can't play without the ball!" Jo called to her.

"Don't interrupt her. She's talking to a B-O-Y," Beck said.

Val heard her teammates laugh. She turned to go.

Tasman grabbed the ball and threw it back toward the team. Then he stood in front of Val to keep her from running after it.

"I'm shocked. Admittedly I only know you in the most superficial way. And I don't know Lanora at all. But I never would have thought you'd be the type of person who abandons her friend when she's in trouble."

"I just told you. She isn't in trouble. She likes those girls," Val said.

"Does she really? Do *you* like those girls?"

Val shook her head.

"And if you don't, then how could they be worth anything? Because you like everybody. Well, almost everybody. After all, you've just said that you don't like them."

Val wiped her face on her shirtsleeve. She wasn't used to people paying this much attention to what she said.

"I wasn't able to find the item you were looking for. But I have something else."

He opened his fist. In the center of his palm was a blue button with only one hole. Two stick figures were indented in the ceramic. One child crawled in one direction. The other in the opposite direction.

"What is it?" Val said.

"It's an amulet. From the First Intermediate period. About 2000 B.C."

She had been about to touch it, but she pulled back her finger. "It's so old."

"Yes. They were often buried with the dead, to protect children."

"Why do you think Lanora needs protection?"

"Don't we all? I mean, the rest of us. You don't, but you can keep it for her." He grabbed her hand and pressed the stone into her palm. Then he closed her fist over the amulet.

She stared at her fist. "I can't take this from you. It's probably really valuable."

"The Captain has dozens. He'll never know it's gone."

The stone grew hot in her hand. That seemed significant, until she realized it was just taking on the warmth from her body. "Won't you get in trouble?"

"When you say 'get in trouble,' you're implying that I'm not already in it."

"Are you in trouble?"

"The human condition is, alas—"

Tasman was interrupted by someone shouting. It didn't sound like the typical boisterous behavior of kids in the park. Val turned to see what was going on.

A man walked unsteadily along the path, mumbling to himself. He wore a ragged blue sheet draped like a toga across one shoulder. It was tied around his waist with a piece of an extension cord. His hair was like a writhing nest of snakes. He carried a pink plastic wand with a star on the end. He waved this wand at the children who gaped at him because they were too young to know they shouldn't stare. It was almost funny. Almost. Sometimes in New York City, you had to laugh so that you wouldn't cry. Val wondered what Tasman thought about the beautiful absurdity of that man with the child's wand.

But Tasman was gone. He had disappeared as completely as if he had never been there. Val opened her hand and stared at the amulet.

The man with the wand bent over to peer at it, too. "Protecting the dead?"

"What?" Val was surprised. How could a man like this possibly know what it was?

He pointed his wand at her accusingly. "What about the living?"

Eleven

L anora luxuriated in her bed long past nine, glad she didn't have to get up and seize the day. She smiled as she stretched. She whispered the word "Saturday," as if it were a foreign language.

Ten years from now, her pajamas would be silk and her sheets would be silk and her comforter would be made from the softest down. When she awoke, the sun would be shining through the ivory gauze of the floor-to-ceiling drapes. She would smell deliciously flavored coffee brewing in a very smart pot that sensed the moment she wanted it. She would pour a cup of that deliciously flavored coffee and take it out onto her terrace. She would hear the sound of birds singing. The wind would toy with a set of chimes. She would sit on her bamboo chair and sip and smile, and be glad that everything in her world was the way it was supposed to be.

Lanora brushed her hair slowly and firmly. The bristles invigorated her scalp. A few curls had reappeared right along her hairline. She didn't want to blow-dry her hair today, so she smoothed it back into a ponytail. She put on her robe. It wasn't silk, but it had red piping along the lapels.

As she walked to the kitchen, she heard music playing in her mom's bedroom. The sorrowful songs all sounded the same. A female voice complained how he'd done her wrong.

Lanora sighed and tightened the belt on her robe. She decided to fix a special brunch for her mom. She got two matching blue mugs, the sugar bowl, and the cream pitcher. It was important never to put the milk carton on the table. She looked in the cupboard for something she could make that wasn't cereal. She spread peanut butter on slices of bread, trimmed off the crusts, and cut them into triangles. She garnished the plates with orange wedges. Then she arranged everything on the table in the most pleasing way.

"Oh, look what you've done. This is so pretty." Emma sat across from her daughter and stirred sugar into her tea.

Lanora smiled. She was glad her mom noticed. Not everybody did.

"It's nice you don't have to rush off to school, isn't it? And I don't have to go to work. We can sit here in our robes." Emma's lavender robe was faded and her slippers had worn toes. She said she didn't need new ones, but Lanora suspected that Emma wanted to wear the things Lanora's father had bought her.

Lanora was never going to cling to the past. She was going to create the best of all possible lives. Excellence was out there. All she had to do was make it.

"It's going okay? School?" Emma said.

"Oh, yes. It's going quite well."

"You like your teachers?"

Lanora raised one eyebrow. This was something she was practicing.

"You don't like your teachers?" Emma said.

"I prefer my friends." She smiled as she said the word because, of course, that word meant something different to someone like her mom.

"The three girls you told me about?"

Lanora stirred her tea. Actually there were four now. Another girl had started hanging around the A Team. Her name was April. Lanora had been surprised that April joined them. April was not A-caliber material. She was so shallow, in fact, that Lanora wondered whether April presented another kind of test, just like the so-called shopping. Alicia had watched Lanora quite closely when Ariel had asked April if she had any plans for the weekend and April had said, "You know." And then they all smiled, as if they did know. So Lanora had smiled, too.

If there were a competition for intelligence or taste or strength, then Lanora had no doubt which of them would win. But she didn't want to ride into battle today. She didn't care what the others were doing. She deserved a treat. These empty hours were a blank canvas.

"Saturday," she whispered to the rim of her mug.

"What are you going to do today?" Emma said.

Lanora nibbled around the perimeter of her sandwich to preserve its shape for as long as possible. What should she do? Visit the castle in Central Park? She always loved climbing the tower, but it was only three stories. Even if you considered the height of the cliff, it wasn't nearly exhilarating enough. Maybe Times Square? The wild lights throbbed with energy. But so many tourists went there. Lanora didn't want to be annoyed by people who had no idea where they were going. Rockefeller Center? Lanora loved the golden statue of Prometheus being given the gift of fire. But that was too near to her father's office. Sometimes he worked on Saturdays. And even if he weren't actually there, that part of the city still belonged to him.

"Are you going to see Val?"

"Val?" Lanora put down her sandwich.

"You do still see Val, don't you?"

"Of course. All the time." That wasn't a lie. Lanora did see Val in the halls at school and sometimes on the street. Those encounters were never easy. Sometimes when she saw her, she wanted to run up to her and hug her. Sometimes she wanted to grab her hand and drag her to the Bower and tell her everything, every thought, every feeling. But she couldn't. No matter how tempting, Lanora had to stick to her plan. She had to treat Val like a relic from an ancient civilization. A piece of the past to be put in safekeeping until it was useful again.

She washed the dishes and went to get dressed. She decided to wear her black-and-yellow jacket. It was her favorite even though it wasn't at all appropriate for school.

The phone rang as she was buttoning her blouse.

"Oh, it's you," Emma said.

Of course. Lanora's father wanted a progress report. He wanted to hear about her test scores and the praise scribbled in the margins of her essays. She had a different kind of triumph in mind. She intended to rule the world—at least her corner of it. She put on her jacket, smoothed her hair, and walked past her mom.

"See you later," she said when she was halfway out the door.

"Wait. Your father wants to talk to you."

"Why? We've only had two weeks of school. I haven't gotten any grades yet."

Lanora walked briskly down Broadway. She hadn't decided on a destination; she would know it when she got there. In the meantime, she enjoyed the sensation of purposefully striding along, passing everyone, crossing streets even when the sign said DON'T WALK.

And then a little troop of fairies skipped across the sidewalk. Their dresses were made of gossamer dragonfly wings. Their hair was pinned up with remnants of the Milky Way. Their feet danced in slippers made from rose petals. They twirled until their skirts lifted them above the ground.

Lanora clapped her hands with delight. She extended her arms to the fairies. But their minders herded them across the plaza and into the opera house.

"Hurry up, girls. We don't want to be late for *Sleeping Beauty*."

She sat on the rim of the fountain. When she was seven, her father had brought her and her mom to the ballet at Lincoln Center. She was so excited to see magic come to life. She barely even noticed all the times he slipped away from them in the dark.

Something glittered on the ground. She picked up a crystal earring. It would have been perfect for the Collection of Magical Devices. She wondered who had the red velvet box. Was it at Val's? Or was it in her own closet? She held the earring up toward the sunshine. Its cut edges made sparkles dance across her other hand.

Then she saw them. The A Team. With April. All four

girls were looking at her. Lanora quickly dropped the earring.

They said, "Hi, Lanora." Like, we see you. You may have thought you fooled us. But now we know you are someone who picks up trash and pretends it's a star.

"You dropped your earring," Alicia said.

Anna kicked it closer to Lanora's foot.

Lanora made her mouth smile at them even as her eyes searched out details. Why were they there? What could she find against them? As usual they were immune to criticism. That was how they lived their lives.

"Don't you want it anymore?" Ariel said.

"Maybe she wants new earrings," Alicia said.

"Earrings are easy to get," Anna said.

"Even *she* could get earrings," Alicia said.

Lanora stood up. She rose to that challenge. "Are you going 'shopping' now?" Lanora said the word in the special way.

"No," Alicia said. Like how could Lanora be so dumb.

"We have tickets to a show at Lincoln Center." April showed Lanora the colorful rectangles. She spread them out so that Lanora could easily count. One, two, three, four.

Lanora looked down at her feet so she wouldn't have to watch them walk away. There was the crystal earring. She stepped on it as hard as she could. She wanted to smash it into nonexistence. So that it would never again tempt anyone to pick it up and imagine it could be transformed into something else.

It didn't break.

"Who cares," she said.

People passed by. No one said, "I care." No one said, "You have to care." No one warned her that when she stopped caring, that was the beginning of the end.

Twelve

Someone was in the closet. Mau opened one eye. She could hear the sound of a crate being dragged along a shelf. Had she miscalculated? Was it time for Tasman to put food in her dish? Her nostrils quivered. Sadly, no. The smell was not of kibble but of old straw, dried-up mouse droppings, and dust from the desert. She wondered why he was opening one of the Captain's boxes. She decided to go find out. She jumped down from the shelf and padded over to the closet. The door was shut. She scratched at the outside.

Tasman quickly opened it. "Be quiet," he hissed.

Mau came inside. It was dark. The boy hadn't turned on a light. His arm was inside the crate. Mau heard the rustle of straw as his fingers patted different objects. He got quite excited and pulled something out. When he saw it was a vase, his arm drooped with disappointment.

"It isn't here," he whispered.

Mau blinked. She didn't care about his futile search. After all, the bag of food was there. She rubbed against it. He didn't give her a handful, as he often did. The boy was not usually immune to her demands, like the Captain. She swatted Tasman's leg. He didn't even look at her. Clearly something was not as it should be. Mau sat down and stared at him until he looked at her.

"It isn't here," he said again. His voice cracked with emotion.

He wiped his nose with the back of his sleeve. He returned the vase to the crate, closed it up, and shoved it back in its place.

Mau scratched the side of the bag of kibble.

"Shh," Tasman warned her again. He put his ear to the closet door. He heard nothing. But Mau wasn't the least bit surprised when Tasman opened the door and discovered the Captain standing there.

"What are you doing?" the Captain said.

Tasman straightened himself up. He was actually as tall as the Captain, even though he never seemed to be.

"I was searching for the . . ." He paused.

"For what?" the Captain said.

Mau looked at one and then the other. The humans didn't usually stare at each other like this. As still and as silent as if they were cats. But they weren't cats, of course, and so eventually they would return to the babble of conversation.

The boy broke first. "I was searching for something I need."

"What?"

"It's just something I need. It isn't important."

The Captain pushed Tasman aside and went into the closet. Mau followed and scratched again at the bag of food, even though she knew it was futile. The Captain pointed to the crate. "What were you doing in there?"

"Aren't they my things? Didn't Grandfather send them with me when he told you to look after me?"

"Yes, they're yours. But they aren't for you to muck around with. I'm keeping them in trust for you. I know the value. I know when to sell. You don't know anything."

"I know more than you think," Tasman muttered.

"Don't I give you what you need? Food, clothes, spending money. Don't I pay you for the work you do? When you do it."

"I'm going to write the new catalogue entries."

The Captain folded his arms across his chest. "I know you took the amulet."

Tasman went back to his desk. "What amulet?"

"The one you took! You think I don't know what's in my own shop? The blue faience one with the two crawling kids."

"Oh. That amulet."

"That amulet. That amulet." The Captain mocked Tasman. He slammed the closet door shut. Mau had to jump quickly to save the tip of her tail.

"How much did you get? You probably got cheated. Did you take it to that crook on the East Side?"

"I didn't sell it." Tasman got out a pen and paper and started writing.

"Didn't sell it? Tarnation. Then why on earth would you steal it from me?"

Tasman's writing got more agitated until the pen slashes ripped the paper. "It's all stolen, isn't it? Everything in here, every vase, every book, every bead, every astrolabe, every bowl was stolen, wasn't it?"

"Bah." The Captain waved his hand and leaned against his desk. "Don't be getting all ethical on me."

Tasman threw down the pen and stomped over to the Captain. "Maybe that's what happened to him. Did you ever think that? Maybe stealing the incantation bowl set the demons loose and caused all the trouble?"

"There isn't a bowl." The Captain banged his fist against his desk. His nostrils flared as he struggled to breathe. When his face wasn't quite so red, he waved his hand and sat down. "That's just a story. Besides. We're not talking about what I've got. We're talking about what I don't have.

What you took." He picked up a letter. "I got an order for that amulet. So you'd better give it back."

Tasman shook his head.

"Blast you. Why not?"

"I gave it to someone who needs it," Tasman said.

The Captain took hold of Tasman's hand and peered sadly into the boy's eyes. "You didn't give it to *him*, did you?"

"No!" Tasman jerked away and hurried back to his desk. "I gave it to Val."

"Who's Val?"

Tasman's face reddened. He shut his notebook and held it close to his chest.

"That girl who was here?" The Captain spluttered. "You could have given her one of the imitations. She wouldn't know the difference."

"I know the difference," Tasman said.

"That's what worries me. You've got a lot of nonsense in your head. If you start believing the things you write for the catalogue, you can get in a lot of trouble."

"I'm already in trouble," Tasman muttered.

"What?" the Captain said.

Tasman picked up his pen and bent over his notebook.

Mau sat outside the door to the closet, waiting patiently for food to appear in her dish and for all to be right with the world.

Thirteen

For over a month, black-and-white posters had haunted the bus stops. Young, beautiful people in beautiful, angular poses with no explanation of who or what they were—except that the letter Q, X, or R appeared somewhere in the photo. Then, on Sunday, a new clothing store opened up right around the corner from M.S. 10. It had a distinctive red sign with the initials *QXR* carelessly scrawled in black.

Lanora hadn't gone to the new store right away. She liked delaying gratification. She liked having power over everything—including her desires. But she expected that the A Team would want to go on Monday.

All day she planned that shopping expedition. If they wanted her to get earrings, then she would get earrings.

But the A Team had other plans for after school. They were going to a new program that April had told them about.

"Too bad you don't go to the *école spéciale*," Alicia said.

The members of the A Team made a small pout with their lips. The French called that expression a *faire la moue*. Lanora already knew what that meant—I'm not sorry even though I'll pretend to be.

"Who needs more school," she said, knowing full well it wasn't school. It was enjoying pastries and cafe au lait. It was learning French pronunciations that made even ordinary words like "chocolate" sound wonderful. It was Alicia, Ariel, Anna, and April riding off together in a big, black town car.

Lanora headed in the opposite direction, without waiting to see if any of them would flick her fingers in farewell. She walked as if she were late for a very important appointment with a magazine editor who wanted Lanora's ideas about what the next trend would be. The sound of her hard heels against the sidewalk ticked off the things that she no longer cared about.

At the top of that list was the A Team.

2. Being quizzed about her emotional state by her mom.
3. Homework.
4. Messages from her father about homework.
5. The shoebox containing the Collection of Magical Devices.

6. All her colorful clothes, including the black-and-yellow jacket, which had been stained by the sweat of humiliation on Saturday.

Her list grew longer, not by addition but by multiplication. Her mind raced with more and more items she disdained.

7. People walking slowly.
8. People walking slowly pushing babies in strollers.
9. Cute dogs with perky ears.
10. Ugly dogs that were supposed to be cute.
11. DON'T WALK signs.

The only way to stop the list from exploding into exponents was to slam on the brakes and say "whatever."

Then there it was. QXR. The door was open. The store wanted her to come in. Music pulsed into the street. The lights gleamed. Window displays tempted her with new visions of herself. The intense air-conditioning promised a world without sweat.

But she walked on by. She needed to prepare herself. She knew that if you wanted something desperately, you wouldn't get it. She had observed that the more her mom begged her father, the faster he ran away. The A Team hadn't taught Lanora anything she didn't already know.

She paused in front of another store. She checked her hair in the window that was as good as a mirror. She saw something worse than a straggling curl; she saw Val standing on the opposite side of Broadway. Val stared at Lanora like Val was trying to solve an algebra problem. Give it up, Lanora wanted to tell her. You'll never understand. You don't want things the way I want things. You don't need to.

Lanora hardened her face and retraced her steps. She wasn't going to speak to Val. She wouldn't even look at her. Not even if a lion escaped from the zoo and snatched Val up in his mouth. Lanora added Val to the list of things she no longer cared about.

The door to QXR was open. Lanora crossed the threshold and entered a new world. Her heart pounded with excitement. But she sidled over to a rack of uninspiring jeans. She flipped through them with one hand, even as her mind danced around all the dazzling possibilities.

What should she choose? Leather bags. Golden jewelry. Shimmering silks. She had to decide quickly. Hesitation would bring the unwelcome attention of a clerk. Lanora moved on from the jeans. She passed a table of small stuffed animals. She smiled as she stroked a little black cat. The plush fur was almost as comforting as a real animal's. She let her hand linger while she planned what to do. The task wasn't difficult. She had seen the A Team succeed many times. She just wanted to choose the right item. It would belong to her forever.

Val wondered why Lanora had walked into the store with her jaw set, like she was going into battle. Val had hoped Lanora would be proud of herself for dumping the A Team. Val wanted to rush up to her and cheer, Yay, you did it! You broke your spell!

Only Val couldn't after Lanora disappeared inside the new store.

When had it opened? Had it sprung up overnight? For nearly a year, Val had seen the GOING OUT OF BUSINESS signs in the funny little shops. Pet food, candles, what was the other one? Val couldn't remember. All had vanished, despite her mom attending community meetings and signing petitions and even threatening to chain herself to the door of the candle shop.

Val wasn't exactly forbidden to go inside QXR. Just like Val wasn't exactly forbidden to shave her head. Her mom just assumed that she wouldn't want to. And Val didn't. She only wanted to talk to Lanora. She wasn't dumb enough to think that Lanora was the good old Lanora just because Lanora was no longer friends with the A Team. But Lanora might have wanted to know that the school janitor kept a pet snail in a coffee cup. Or that Drew had decided that he was left-handed. Or about this strange boy Tasman who also knew Mau.

Val took a deep breath, as if she were about to dive into the ocean, and entered. Immediately she was assaulted by frigid air, loud mechanical music and glaring lights. She stopped just past the security guard. Where was Lanora? Val couldn't tell. Versions of the new Lanora were everywhere. The girls scrutinizing the clothes on the racks. The mannequins stuck to the walls. The shop clerks leaning against the counters.

One sidled over to Val and said, "Can I help you?"

Val knew she meant the opposite. "Can I help you?" meant "I can't help you." Meant "I won't help you." "You are beyond help."

Well, Val was in her baggy shorts and her Pelé T-shirt. Her running shoes were scuffed. Her only jewelry was a collection of strings that Drew had tied around her wrist that morning as he told her about *his* string theory. The real one, not the astronomical one their dad tried to explain at dinner last night.

"Can I help you?" the clerk said again.

"No," Val said.

The clerk raised her eyebrows and slouched back to one of the other clerks. They whispered to each other.

Val stuck her hand in her pocket. The amulet Tasman had given her was still there. She traced its indentation with her finger. Should she give it to Lanora? Would Lanora want it? Its powers seemed overwhelmed by everything else in this store.

Then Val spotted Lanora standing by a jewelry display. Lanora seemed mesmerized by the glitter. Gold and silver deflected the light like a multitude of little mirrors. Lanora touched an earring with her index finger. When it spun, it sent a shiver of light. Then she stopped that motion by clutching the disk in her fist. She seemed to struggle against a desire. But what kind? Why didn't she let go of the earring? Was she going to take it?

"Lanora, don't!" Val's voice was louder than the electronic drumbeats.

Lanora dropped the earring and quickly moved away from the spot. She wasn't fast enough to escape the attention of the security guard and the store manager.

They surrounded Lanora and pushed her back against a table piled high with precisely folded T-shirts.

"What's in your bag?" the guard said.

Val picked up the gold disk and brought it over to show the guard. "Here's the earring. She didn't put it in her bag. She just dropped it." Val was so happy that she had saved her friend from a terrible fate.

The manager stuck her hand inside Lanora's book bag. The manager smiled as she pulled out a fuzzy black cat wearing the store's distinctive red tag with the QXR scrawl.

"You'd better come with us," the manager said.

Val watched in horror as the guard dragged Lanora to the back of the store. The manager carried the cat by its tail.

Lanora didn't look at Val. Not once. Val didn't think Lanora would ever look at her again.

Fourteen

Val waited outside the store. At any moment she expected Lanora to come out, laughing because it was all a big mistake. The toy cat had fallen into her bag by accident. What a funny joke.

Only Lanora didn't come out. Lanora's mom rushed in. Still, Val managed to keep hoping that everything would be okay until she saw a policewoman march into the store. Then Val slowly went home.

Drew tackled her the minute she came in the apartment. "You are my prisoner. I'm taking you to my secret lair so you can do my boring homework sheet while I save the world, or at least the parts I like."

He tried to lift her. Usually she stood on her tiptoes so that he could feel as if he had succeeded. Her body felt too heavy to move. Like she had been encased in cement so her head wouldn't explode. It throbbed with everything she was trying not to think.

What had happened? She had been at the store. She had seen Lanora. Val had seen the little toy cat. And yet she still didn't know.

Drew let go of her. He poked her in all her ticklish places—including the one behind her left knee. She didn't laugh. He frowned. He dragged over a chair and climbed up so he could peer in her eyes.

"Aha! It's as I suspected. You are *not* my sister Valerie Braun. You were *not* born on April 23rd. You do *not* live at 255 West 83rd Street. You are an impostor!"

He ran into his room and came out with a plastic sword. He pointed the blade at her neck. "Tell me what you've done with my sister or I'll cut off your head."

"Go ahead." Val was happy to be punished for something.

Drew's eyes widened. Then he dropped the sword and ran into the kitchen. "Mommy, something's wrong with Val!"

Mom came out holding a wooden spoon in one hand with the other cupped beneath it to catch the red drips. "Don't you feel good?"

No, Val wanted to cry. She wanted to bury her face in her mom's soft sweater and tell her everything. But what could Val say? Wasn't it tattling to say Lanora had stolen the cat? Even if it wasn't, could Val say how she knew this? Worst of all, how could she ever explain that she was the reason Lanora got caught? Val couldn't. She could only shrug.

Drew raced into his room and raced back out carrying his doctor's kit—a big, black satchel with bottles containing eyes of newts, fish teeth, and other potions so powerful that they could change into whatever he decided he needed them to be.

"I, the great Hyper Condriack, will cure you. Open your mouth and take these pills."

He tried to stick his finger into her mouth. But she had to keep her lips pressed together. She couldn't let her little brother see her cry. She pushed him away and walked into her room. Even with the door shut, she could hear their voices.

"Mommy, why won't she let me doctor her?"

"Maybe you should help me cook instead."

"This is no time for food. I have to cure Val."

"She's pretty resourceful. I think she can cure herself. Come on. You can add the spices."

"Okay. If I can use some of my superpotions."

"Use whatever you want, so long as it's basil and oregano."

Val took the amulet out of her pocket. She turned it over and over in her hand. No matter which way she looked at it, the children inscribed in the circle still crawled off in opposite directions.

Drew set the table. The dishes were sort of in the right spots. But he had dumped the silverware in a heap in the center next to a dish of frozen peas.

"What's that?" Dad said, pointing at the peas.

"A center peas. Get it? Get it?" Drew said to Val.

"I get it." Val tentatively took one bite. Then she put down her fork and sighed.

"Is there something wrong with the zucchini?" Mom said.

"Yes! They are vegetables! Get it? Get it?" Drew said.

"Who wound you up?" Dad said.

"Val," Drew said.

"No, I didn't," Val said.

"Yes, you did. You're so quiet, I have to make four times as much noise as I usually do."

Dad laughed. Mom did too, but only for a moment. Then she said to Drew, "Why don't you tell us what happened at school?"

"You mean at superhero academy?" Drew said.

"Yes," Mom said.

Val kept her head down as if she were eating.

"Since most of the time we are learning things I already know, like reading and writing, I get to spend my time practicing my powers."

"Are you sure that's a good thing?" Dad said.

"Oh, yes. Powers come in very handy. When you least expect it. Like now, for instance. At our very own dinner table. When you might think I could be relaxing and eating my dinner, instead I am having to use my special power of resbo-noitva."

"Do you mean 'observation'?" Mom said.

Drew rolled his eyes and shook his head. "No. I had to look at things from the inside out to find what's wrong with Val."

"Nothing is wrong." Val wished she could kick him under the table like she used to. Unfortunately her parents had gotten a round table so she couldn't reach his legs without sliding halfway down her chair.

"Yes, there is. You've got what Lanora's got," Drew said.

Val glared at Drew. But he wouldn't shut up.

"What's that?" Dad said.

"The great evil Werd, who has my name spelled backwards, has put a spell on them both! Don't worry. I'm more powerful than my nemesis. I will save the day."

The phone rang.

"I'll get it, I'll get it," Drew shouted. "It's probably Werd calling to taunt me from his secret lair, ha ha ha!"

Dad put his hand on Drew to keep him in his seat.

Mom left the table to grab the phone. "Why, Emma. How nice to hear from you."

There was only one reason Lanora's mom would call. Val stared at her plate. She watched red glop ooze away from the pasta. She tried to push it back with her fork.

"Oh. How awful," Mom said.

"What's awful?" Drew whispered.

The red glop won. It contaminated the garlic bread. The best part of the dinner was ruined.

"I'm so sorry to hear it," Mom said.

"Hear what?" Drew whispered.

"Stop listening. It's rude." Val slid down in her chair until she could kick him. She felt like slipping all the way to the floor.

"She's just gotten into a little trouble. That happens. But she's still a wonderful girl," Mom said.

Emma's voice could be clearly heard. "She didn't even say she was sorry!"

That was true. Lanora had not said she was sorry, no matter how many times her mom complained. Lanora couldn't manage the phrase in any form—not even a mumble of the main word. Lanora didn't think she needed to apologize to anyone. And yet, she actually was sorry.

Sorry her mom had called Val's mom. Sorry that the TV in the cab hadn't filled the angry silence. Sorry she had been squished in the backseat between her parents. Sorry her father had whined about leaving an important appointment to meet them at the juvenile center. Sorry her mom kept trying to find out if the appointment was with a new girlfriend or the same one. Sorry the juvenile center had buzzing fluorescent lights. Sorry the policewoman had a chicken pox scar right between her eyes. Sorry they searched her pockets to make sure she hadn't taken anything besides the cat. Sorry they kept the cat. Sorry a poor person in a poor country had worked so hard to make that black, fuzzy cat. Sorry Val had been in the store to see all that. Sorry Lanora had ever been born.

Fifteen

On Tuesday, the news ricocheted around the hallways at school, bouncing off the lockers and the inspirational messages on the bulletin boards. Lanora had been arrested. Lanora was in jail. Lanora was in a psych ward. The only ones who weren't discussing Lanora were the members of the A Team. Even the janitor, pushing his broom to sweep up the gum wrappers, the lost homework, and the hair ties, shook his head about this kind of mess.

During lunchtime, the Poetry Club sat in their customary circle on the floor. When Val came in, they were just finishing a moment of silence—for them, a rare tribute indeed.

"Lanora, Lanora, Lanora." They spoke her name as if it were an obituary.

"When I first met her, she was reading this book." Helena opened her own copy of Emily Brontë poems and started to read.

"'Well, some may hate and some may scorn/And some may quite forget thy name/But my sad heart must ever mourn/Thy ruined hopes, thy blighted fame.'"

"Don't read that," Val interrupted.

"She objects to rhymes?" Tina said.

"Many do," Olivia said.

"Especially A B A B," Gillian said.

"A B C B would have been an improvement," Tina said.

"I don't care about the rhymes. The poem is so harsh. Like her life is over. When it isn't," Val said.

"It isn't?" Helena said.

"Not technically," Tina said.

"Not at all." Val pounded on the floor.

They all looked at her expectantly.

"She feels bad for her former friend," Olivia said.

"If only Lanora had chosen soccer as a hobby." Gillian kicked an imaginary ball with her boot.

"Instead she picked lifting." Tina spread her hands.

Val opened her lunch bag. She tried to be happy her mom had stopped giving her grapes. But the apple reminded her of Lanora, too. Val crumpled the bag.

"Aren't you hungry?" Olivia said.

Val shook her head. None of the poets felt the same way she did. Lanora had never been their friend. And none of them were directly responsible for getting Lanora in trouble.

"Aha." Helena pointed her finger in the air. "I have solved all the problems. Rhyme and sentiment." She cleared her throat and spoke. "'Well, some may hate and some may scorn/And some may quite forget thy name/But loyal Val will rectify/Thy ruined hopes, thy blighted fame.'"

Those words echoed in Val's head for the rest of the day. Each time she heard someone snigger about Lanora the lifter, Val became even more determined. Yes, she would rectify Lanora! Who else but loyal Val would?

After school, she told her teammates she couldn't go to soccer practice. There was something she had to do. She spoke with confidence, even though she didn't know how she would accomplish the task. Or even exactly what it was.

Val walked slowly to the horrible QXR store. She stood outside the window, watching the store manager watch the security guard watch the customers. Her mom would have marched inside to complain about unlawful searches and seizures. Her dad would have pranked them by trying to purchase lots of expensive items with monopoly money. Her brother would have smushed his face against the glass and left a great gob of snot for the store manager to clean up. But Val knew that rectifying Lanora was more complicated than revenge.

The word, she found out when she looked it up during

ELA, meant to put things right. How could Val put Lanora right? Especially if Val had no idea what was wrong.

The music was giving her a headache. She crossed Broadway. She walked up a few blocks and then back toward the park. She didn't have a destination in mind, but she wasn't completely surprised to find herself standing on the sidewalk staring at a sign that said ANTIQUITIES FROM THE SHIPWRECK OF TIME.

A flock of crows had taken over all the branches of a small tree. Their raucous cries sounded like they were scolding each other. Then one crow opened his beak and stared directly at her.

"I don't believe in spells," she said.

The crows cackled as they spread their wings and flew away.

"I don't," she said again. But she entered the little yard and went to peer in the window. The wedjat winked as the sign swung back and forth. She barely noticed it. *The Book of Dares* was gone. In its place was a stone head whose nose had been chiseled off.

"Tarnation, where's the packing material?" she heard the Captain shout.

Tasman answered, "Where it always is."

"Then we've run out. Bah. Won't get that book shipped today."

Was he sending away *The Book of Dares*? How would she ever find out what to do? The gate was shut, but not locked. She pushed it open. The hinges creaked. She slipped through the opening and entered the store.

The aisles were blocked with even more stacks of old books, making a maze that only the smartest of lab rats would have been able to figure out. She wandered through the store. She hoped to find Tasman before the Captain found her.

"Did you do that catalogue entry?" the Captain said.

"I'm working on it," Tasman said.

"Reading the books, you mean," the Captain said.

"Don't I have to do research?" Tasman said.

"Bah. Just make it up. No one will notice," the Captain said.

She followed the sounds of Tasman's voice. Finally, in the gap between two boxes, she spotted a blue boot. She reached between the boxes to touch it.

Tasman jumped up in surprise. When he saw her, he grinned excitedly.

Val put her finger to her lips. She took his notebook and wrote: "I have to talk to you. Come outside."

He nodded. He shut his notebook. She saw the cover was decorated with a unicorn. Obviously he didn't go to public school. If he carried that down the halls of M.S. 10, he'd be dead. Val wondered if he were being homeschooled. But he wasn't at home, he was in a shop. Had he been kicked out of school? Or had he just never gone?

He was beckoning to her. She followed him down a different aisle. They both crouched to keep their heads below the top of the boxes.

"Tasman?" the Captain called.

"I'm going to get packing material," Tasman said.

He opened the gate. She stepped outside. He clanged it shut.

"This is so amazing. I was thinking about you, and you appeared! I might have powers that are hidden even to myself. Of course we'll ignore the other times when I was thinking about you and you didn't appear. Wait, wait. We won't ignore them. We'll explain them in a different way. Perhaps I needed to be thinking about you while doing something else. Although in this case, I'm not sure what that would be. I know. I was digesting my lunch. I'm sorry. I'm so excited, I'm not making sense. You've come for your own reason—not mine."

"Lanora was arrested for shoplifting," Val said.

He opened his mouth and then closed it without saying anything.

"It's my fault she was caught. I saw her about to take something. So I called her name, to warn her. Only she had already lifted a toy cat. It's so stupid to do that. Her father is rich. She could have bought a hundred. She must be under a spell."

"So that's why you came. You want the book after all."

"But it's gone. Is the Captain sending it away?"

They both turned to look at the window. The stone head stared back at them with empty eyes.

"Maybe."

"We have to get it. I don't know what else to do," Val said.

Tasman seemed to think for a moment. "You would just go take it? You wouldn't be afraid?"

"I wouldn't take it. I would borrow it. And no, I'm not afraid of the Captain. Not really," Val said.

"I mean, afraid of doing a spell," Tasman said.

"No," Val said. "Are you?"

He laughed. "I'm afraid of everything. And nothing. But mostly afraid of . . ."

"What?" Val whispered.

"It'll be okay. I know how to protect us. I know what we need to get."

"What kind of thing? Is it hard to find?"

"It's in the shop. At least, I'm fairly certain it's in the shop."

The Captain's face appeared at the window. He selected one of the small cat-lady statues and returned to the shadows of the shop.

"I'd better go," Tasman said.

"Wait. What thing are you talking about?" Val said.

Tasman shook his head. "It isn't important." He said it in such a way that Val knew it was the most important thing in the world.

She took his hand and pulled him out of the yard. "Come on. I know a better place for us to talk."

He let her lead him until they were on the sidewalk. Then they dropped hands because Val walked a little bit faster and in more of a straight line than he did.

"Are you going to tell me where we're going? Or is the name of the place unknown or unpronounceable or death to those who say it?"

"The Bower," Val said.

"The Bower. That's most unusual," he said.

"Lanora thought of it after her father took her to see some Shakespeare."

"She's lucky to have a father like that."

"She doesn't anymore. Her parents got divorced. Then he changed jobs. He moved to the East Side. So he never comes around."

"The East Side!" He placed his hands alongside his face in mock horror.

They left the side street. Now that they were on the avenue, they had to dart around people pushing strollers and dragging dogs.

"What would it be like if human variations were as extreme as the different kinds of dogs? If those ladies were poodles and those guys were labs and those guys were pit bulls and those girls . . ."

He stopped talking and walking.

"What?" Val said.

"My train of thought crashed into a brick wall. Cars derailed. Countless casualties. Happy journeys cut short."

"Why?"

"I looked into the eyes of some girls who somehow communicated the concept that I am a worthless waste of time."

Val looked over her shoulder. From behind, Val couldn't see their faces but she recognized that sleek hair. "They're the worthless ones."

"Do you know them?" he said.

"No. Those are Lanora's new friends. Or they were. They dropped her."

"They took her to the wilderness and abandoned her? You're right. It is very important that you bring her back."

They crossed the last street. Mau sat on the wall that surrounded the park.

"It's like she's expecting us," Val said.

"She probably is," Tasman said.

"How would she know I was bringing you to the Bower?" Val said.

"Maybe she's been communing with the universe," Tasman said.

"Or maybe she's just being a cat."

Val climbed on top of the wall. Tasman hesitated.

"There is a gate, if you don't want to climb," Val said.

"You didn't say the Bower was in the park."

"Why don't you like the park?"

He stared at Val. She smiled. She offered him her hand. He didn't move. She sighed and jumped down from the wall.

"I guess we can go someplace else," Val said.

"No. Wait. I can do it. You'll be with me. If ever there were a time, it would be now." He climbed up the wall. He struggled to find the places for his feet. But he made it. He stood on top triumphant. Then he carefully looked right and left and then right and left again. Finally he jumped down.

Val quickly followed. She led him to the top of the large rocks. He carefully searched in all directions before sitting down beside her.

"Tell me about this thing," Val said.

Tasman patted the gray rock. "This is schist. It's so hard because it was formed by pressure deep within. A metaphoric, metamorphic rock."

"Do you deliberately refuse to answer questions? Or are *you* under a spell?" Val said.

He didn't speak. She tried to see his face. His eyes were hidden by his hair. The distant sounds of children playing only made him more agitated. He placed his hands on the rock with his fingers spread wide. He took three deep breaths. Then he said, "It's an incantation bowl."

"What is that?" Val said.

"A rare artifact from the Middle East. Most were made in the fifth or sixth century. They are inscribed with words that spiral down to the center of the bowl. The words are an incantation. An invocation. A kind of a prayer."

"For what?" Val said.

"To trap the demon."

"You think Lanora has a demon?"

"No."

"Then why do you want the bowl?"

He shut his eyes and took a deep breath. "Once, long ago, there was an archaeologist who journeyed to the Middle East."

From the shadows, Mau crept closer as if to listen to the story.

"He didn't have as many camels and assistants as the men from the more prestigious universities, but he did have a more vivid imagination. That helped him find treasures other men could only envy."

"He must be related to you." Val playfully punched his shoulder.

Tasman glared at her accusingly. "What are you talking about?"

"It's a compliment. The man had a great imagination. And so do you."

"Oh. That's what you meant." He tried to smile. He couldn't. So he continued. "He found the typical scrolls and scarabs and shards and little blue faience hippopotami. He dutifully sent all those things back to his sponsors. All except one item that he found in the Desert of Nippur. A bowl."

"*The* bowl?"

"He knew he shouldn't keep it. He knew he should leave it buried in the ground, so that it could continue to do its work to protect that family against their demons." Tasman's face got very red. He picked up a stick and broke it.

"But he kept it?"

Tasman nodded. "He had a son who was very sick. Who saw what no one else could see. The son's visions were so frightening that he stayed in his room and refused to come out. There is medicine to sedate people like that. He was supposed to take the pills. Only he was afraid."

"Of what? Didn't he want to be well?"

"He was afraid that if he ever took his eyes off those demons, they would get him."

A wind rustled the leaves in a nearby tree. At least that was what they hoped made the sound.

"What happened next?" Val said.

"The archaeologist took the bowl and wrapped it in special cloth. He packed it in his trunk, careful to keep it upside down. It traveled by camel, by caravan, by ship, finally reaching the port of New York City. The archaeologist took it to his home on West 129th Street. His son was upstairs, shouting and cursing at the things that no one else could see. The archaeologist buried the bowl upside down in the yard. He said the incantation to trap the demons in the bowl. Then he waited. And waited. All night, he sat. But the words he repeated were drowned out by the shouts of his son as he wrestled with the demons."

"Did it work?"

Tasman sadly shook his head.

"So why do you want the bowl?"

"Sometimes even the thing that doesn't work is better than nothing."

⌒Sixteen⌒

On Wednesday Lanora appeared before the judge. She wore a white blouse and a navy blue skirt. Only her patterned tights reminded her that she was still Lanora. Unfortunately the tights itched. She kept her hands folded so she wouldn't scratch her legs as she sat between her mother and the lawyer.

Her father wasn't there. He had sent the lawyer in his place. The lawyer looked very much like her father. He wore a pale blue tie with his dark gray suit. His hair was cut as short as her father's. The back of his neck was shaved. Black dots showed where hair would have been, without the barber's razor. The lawyer's watch was slightly smaller than her father's. But the main difference between the men was that the lawyer smiled at Lanora. Once he even patted her shoulder, while the judge read out loud what Lanora had done.

It was strange to hear them discussing this Lanora, who had no previous offenses. Who had been tempted by a cute kitty. Who would never, ever do anything like this again. Who was sorry. Who would do community service. And never step inside that store for as long as she lived.

Well, at least that last part was true.

And then it was over. The lawyer shook hands with Lanora and then Emma. He closed his brown briefcase (it was the box kind with metal latches that snapped into place). He hurried from the room to his next appointment.

Lanora hurried, too. She had to wait outside the courtroom for her mom, who was saying an emotional thank-you to the judge.

Once they had escaped from the halls of justice and were standing on the sidewalk, Emma blew her nose and said, "I hope you learned your lesson."

"Oh, sure," Lanora said.

"Don't take that tone with me," Emma said.

Lanora said nothing for the entire subway ride home.

Actually she *had* learned her lesson. Plenty of lessons. She reviewed them when she was safely in her room, as her mom searched the kitchen cupboards for Tension Tamer tea.

"I'm sure we still had some. How could it all be gone?" Emma said.

Lesson 1: Maintain Your Guard.

Don't get tempted by a cat, no matter how adorable and cuddly. Don't let sentiment stick its grubby little fingers in a crack in the door. Don't allow a crack in the door. Don't allow a door. Block it up with bricks.

"I guess it'll have to be black tea. We're probably out of honey, too," Emma said.

Lesson 2: Be Prepared.

If she'd had a good lie, she would have gotten away with it. If she'd said, I only took the kitty for my poor little sister who is dying of cancer. No, that lie was too much. If she'd said, I wanted to cheer up my poor little sister because our parents are getting divorced, that would have totally worked.

"No, there's still a little in the jar. Of course it's as hard as a rock," Emma said.

Lesson 3: Know Who to Blame.

Not Val. Lanora could never blame Val. Val was probably torn up by the whole situation. First that Lanora had lifted something. And second that Val had gotten Lanora caught. Well, Val shouldn't have followed Lanora. But that small misdemeanor was nothing compared to all the crimes committed by a certain individual. He was so guilty; he didn't dare come to court—the judge would have sent him straight to jail.

The tea kettle screamed. "Lanora? Sweetie? Come get your tea!" Emma said.

"In a minute!" Lanora called.

Lesson 4: Harden Your Heart.

She kind of thought she had done that. Wasn't that why she hung around the A Team? They helped her get to the level where she didn't even feel Val looking at her anymore. Oh, yes. Lanora had been untouchable as she walked through the halls of M.S. 10. She would be again. When she returned tomorrow.

She examined her face in the mirror. Her hair was still perfectly sleek. She had gotten up extra early that morning to have time to blow-dry it. But there was something unfortunate about her eyes.

The dark places were still there. She knew they were the pupils. She knew their purpose was to let in light and whatever images were out there in the world. She knew everything except why they had to look like such horrible, big black holes.

She turned away from her mirror, opened her window, and climbed out onto the fire escape.

The days were getting colder. That was a good thing. She liked the air to be brisk. She liked to feel invigorated. She looked up at the lights just starting to come on in the tall building. Soon there would be a sprinkle of stars beyond. She climbed up one step. Then another. And another.

She was in command. As long as she kept climbing. As long as she didn't look down. Or back. There was no point in that. Who would want to remember that moment when she had begged her father not to move away and he had patted her on the head or given her a lollipop or something. And she had crumpled to the floor. Like she had lost control of everything—even her own legs. Who would ever want to think about that except to remind herself.

Lesson 5: Harden Your Heart Even Harder.

~Seventeen~

Starting school the second time was much more difficult than it had been the first.

Lanora felt too nervous to eat the breakfast her mom
insisted upon. Then the cereal got soggy and her mom
wouldn't let her dump it out and pour a new bowl.

She couldn't decide what to wear. The bold skirt and
jagged top she had laid out so carefully the night before
totally failed to express her defiance. Her old clothes
were old. Her new ones reminded her too much of QXR.
In the end, she had settled for black leggings and a black
dress, even though it was the New York cliché.

As she hugged her mom good-bye, she saw her reflec-
tion in the mirror. She tried the smile. The one she would
need to navigate the halls of M.S. 10. Yes, there it was.
The curl of her lip. She still had it. She turned her head
slightly to get a different angle. She saw the piece of her

hair sticking out. One stray curl, as wispy as the feather of a baby robin.

Lanora ducked under her mom's hands. She selected a scissors from her desk organizer. She snipped off the offensive curl and let it fall to the floor. She faced the mirror again. She was ready now.

She really was. But she didn't want to have to stand around waiting for the door to open. She wanted to walk right in, without having time for conversations or explanations. She thought she planned it right, but she must have made a miscalculation.

By the time Lanora arrived, the door was already shut. The guard was gone. The kids were all inside—laughing, talking, probably about her.

She stared at the door. If it opened, she would walk in. It would be a sign. A message from the great beyond. She didn't believe in things like that. She certainly didn't believe that her bad luck had begun when she buried the lilac butterfly at the Bower. She wondered what would happen if she retrieved it. Nothing. Except that she would have in her possession a filthy bit of plush fabric.

The door stayed shut. Those who were in stayed in. Those who had been absent for the past two days (so they could tell a judge how sorry they were that they tried to take another insignificant bit of plush fabric) stayed out.

Lanora looped her fingers through the chain-link fence

and stared at the brick walls. She had heard of a certain kind of bomb, invented by a diabolically clever person, that destroyed people and left the buildings intact.

"Boom," she whispered.

She straightened the strap of her book bag and walked away, as briskly as if she knew exactly where she was going. She made sure her grim smile was in place. If she saw anyone, anyone at all, even the lamest of the losers, she would have to pretend she had recently been hit on the head by a rock and was enjoying amnesia.

She thought she would be safe until lunchtime. After all, she was outside. And every other kid in the city was stuck inside.

She tried to enjoy this freedom. She could go anywhere in New York City! Yippee! Anywhere except her apartment. Or Val's apartment. Or the Bower. In short, anywhere except places where she might have wanted to be.

She tossed her head, gripped her bag, squared her shoulders, and strode down the sidewalk. She turned away from each orange DON'T WALK sign and crossed the street in the other direction. For the next few hours, she allowed fate to guide her. She shouldn't have.

The gang loitering outside the deli were drinking Cokes and eating chips. Lanora checked her phone in surprise. The hours seemed to be passing so slowly, and yet it was lunch-time. The kids might not recognize her. After all, she didn't really know them. When she was part of the A Team, she glided past kids like these. But she wasn't part of the A Team anymore.

The one with the Yankees baseball cap incorrectly colored red pointed at her with his can of Coke. "Look. It's Lanora the lifter," he said.

"Lanora the lousy lifter," another said.

She couldn't retreat. If she showed them she cared, she would never be able to go back to school. But she didn't feel able to walk past them. Her hair wasn't right. Her armpits were sweaty. She had no idea what had happened to her contemptuous smile.

"Hey, Lanora. They let you out of jail?"

"She wasn't in jail."

"She was in the psych ward."

She ducked through the nearest door and entered a hardware store. The shelves were crammed with pots, tools, paintbrushes, and a multitude of things she would never want. She slunk past a large woman sitting on a stool by the entrance. She wandered through the aisles until she found a secluded corner near the back of the store. She could wait there until lunch was over and it would be safe to leave.

Above her was a rack of shiny golden keys. The shiny bits of metal mesmerized her with their possibilities. What treasure chests could she open? She trailed her finger along the keys, keys, keys. The musical jingling brought back the thrill of that other day, in that other store, when she had felt so powerful.

It would be so much easier to go back to school with a golden key. She could wear it on a chain around her neck. Like a medal to show the world she didn't care that she got caught. She had persisted and won the game.

She stroked the keys. The shimmering sound was so magical. But she stopped the vibration so she could listen.

The store was silent. The woman at the front was probably keeping her eye on the things kids usually wanted—spray paint, glue, batteries. The woman at the front didn't know what really mattered. Keys could open doors. Keys could lock them. Keys were proof of ownership. Could there be anything more important?

Lanora glanced left and then right. No one was watching her. Val wasn't here to ruin everything. Lanora looked up to decide. At the very top was a dark gold key with an elegantly curved head. She stood on her tiptoes to take it off the hook. As usual, she knew exactly what she wanted.

At least she thought she did.

Eighteen

As Val came back from lunch, there was a commotion outside the school. A kid Val didn't know very well was telling everybody a story. His red baseball cap was on crooked. His hands were high in the air, as if he were holding on to an imaginary stick.

"The old lady is holding a broom like this. She chases Lanora down the sidewalk and smacks Lanora on the head."

The kids groaned. "Whoa."

Val pushed closer so she could hear. She found herself standing next to the A Team. They were all sipping drinks through green straws.

"*Wham, wham, wham!* The old lady hits Lanora with the broom until she drops what she lifted."

"What was it this time? Another toy?"

"Nope. A key."

The kids all laughed. "Lanora the lame lifter."

The A Team smiled as they turned away.

Val stepped in front of them. "Don't you care that she's in trouble? Wasn't she your friend?"

Alicia raised an eyebrow. "The woman with the broom?"

Ariel tossed her cup toward a trash can that was overflowing with uneaten lunches. The cup missed, of course. The girls kept walking. Like they hadn't done anything. Like they were not responsible. Like even the laws of gravity didn't apply to them.

So Val picked up the cup and tapped Ariel on the shoulder. "You dropped this."

Ariel raised one eyebrow.

April smiled.

Anna tossed back her hair. "She picks up trash."

"Like Lanora." Their lips curled in something that wasn't really a smile.

"What's that supposed to mean?" Val said.

The girls tilted their heads. They never explained. Why should they? They understood themselves perfectly.

The bell rang. They went inside. Val stood there, still holding the cup. It was sticky. She threw it at the trash can. The cup bounced to the sidewalk. Then she had to pick it up again. Then she had to cross the street to throw it in a can that wasn't overflowing with garbage.

By then, she was so angry that she kept going.

The iron gate was locked. Val rattled the bars so fiercely that the wooden sign started to swing. She rapped on the window. Mau was sleeping next to the statue of the man without a nose. She looked up at Val in surprise and then stretched and jumped off the display shelf.

After a few moments, Tasman came to unlock the gate. "What are you doing here? I'm of course glad to see you. But isn't this a school day?"

"They threw a cup on the ground and they didn't pick it up." Val's anger had only increased. She pushed past Tasman and walked through the maze of boxes. "Where's the Captain?"

"He's communing with spirits." Tasman followed after her. "Of the alcoholic variety. He can't be interrupted."

"Good. Then he won't stop us." Val stood on her tiptoes to peer into a crate.

"From doing what?"

"Finding *The Book of Dares* and the incantation bowl."

"Shhh," Tasman said.

It was too late. Those words could not be unsaid. They were too powerful. Too dangerous. Or too loud.

"What's this ruckus?" the Captain shouted.

Tasman grabbed Val's arm and tried to drag her into an

alcove. She shrugged off his hand and waited for the Captain to come.

The Captain had a large, white cloth tied around his neck. He held a chicken leg in one hand and a glass of red wine in the other. "What are you doing here?"

"I came to get *The Book of Dares* and the incantation bowl," Val said.

The Captain waved his chicken leg dismissively. "Bah. No such thing."

"Of course there is. Tasman told me about it."

The Captain glared at Tasman. Tasman looked at his boots.

"I just need to borrow them for my friend," Val said.

"You can't borrow things like that," the Captain said.

"Why not?" Val said.

"Because you don't know what you're doing. Those kind of powers are too easy to abuse." The Captain shook his finger at Tasman. "You of all people should know that some medicine is also a poison."

Tasman shut his eyes.

"Then you should help us use it properly," Val said.

The Captain snorted and took a sip from his wine. "Where did this girl come from again?"

"Mau brought her," Tasman said.

"That good-for-nothing mangy beast."

As if in response, Mau trotted over and sat at the Captain's feet. She stared at the chicken leg.

"Bah." The Captain tossed the leg into a corner. Mau pounced on it. The Captain ripped the cloth from his neck and wiped his hands on it. "I'm a fool to let you talk me into this."

"We can borrow the bowl?" Val said.

Tasman's eyes got wide.

"Not the bowl. *The Book of Dares*." The Captain threw the cloth in the corner and lurched along the aisle toward a glass cabinet.

"But we need the bowl, too," Val said.

"There is no bowl. You hear me? I do not have the incantation bowl." The Captain jabbed his finger at Tasman with each syllable.

There was no sound except the crunch of Mau's teeth as she ate the chicken bone.

Finally Tasman muttered, "I hear you."

The Captain took a key from his pocket and unlocked a glass cabinet. He put on a pair of grimy white gloves. He picked up a thick volume with deckled edges bound in faded red leather. He carefully placed the book on a reading stand.

"I'll give you ten minutes to look at it. But no touching the pages."

"How can we look at it without touching the pages?" Val said.

The Captain gave Tasman a thin brass stick. At one end, a miniature hand pointed its index finger.

Val leaned closer to the book. She couldn't read what was written on the cover. Some of the gold lettering had worn away. The scribbles could have meant anything. What if this old book wasn't what she hoped? And even if it was, could it really help Lanora?

The Captain carefully lifted the thick cover.

Tasman didn't move.

"Come on, then. You're wasting time," the Captain said.

Tasman looked at Val. He took a deep breath. He walked over to the book and flipped the first page with the brass finger.

Standing there, in the shop, surrounded by so many relics, Val thought of how many other people had sought answers from that book. For a thousand years, people had opened it. But how many had found the kind of wisdom that they needed? And how many had found something entirely different?

The pages whispered as Tasman turned them. *Shush, shush, shush,* as if the words imprisoned there rose up from the paper as puffs of smoke. Tasman kept turning pages. Somewhere in the shop, a clock ticked loudly. Val had never noticed it before. She felt her heartbeat bump against the tick, trying to hold back the march of time. Why didn't Tasman hurry?

"What are you looking for? It's all the same gobbledy-gook, isn't it?" the Captain said.

Tasman frowned and flipped three more pages. The brass hand trembled. Then it dropped decisively onto the book. He stopped.

Val glanced at the page. There were no letters or words that she could see. The marks were beautiful, but they didn't look like writing. They reminded her of paths marked on a map. Where they led, she had no idea.

"How are we supposed to read that?" she whispered.

"He reads Latin and Greek," the Captain said.

"It's Aramaic," Tasman said to the Captain. Then Tasman turned to Val. "I will translate. Take some parchment from the table. Write down what I say."

Val picked up a piece of heavy paper and a pen.

Tasman shut his eyes and held his hands a few inches above the pages. He bowed his head. Then he opened his eyes and started to read.

"'Be gracious to me, Providence and Psyche, as I dare to call upon these mysteries to save one of your children.'"

The words rolled off his tongue in an unfamiliar voice. He read as the ancients might have done, standing in a temple, trying to be heard by the moon.

"'First, I restore to you a gift from the gods, that my message to you may travel with all possible speed.'"

Val wrote as quickly as she could. She wished she dared

to ask him to slow down, but she didn't think he could control what he was doing. The words came unbidden.

"'Second, I bring to you a gift from the Star Tamer, who from his great heights has given proof of his devotion to our cause.'"

Gradually her writing began to flow. Transforming sounds to symbols became part of the ceremony, too.

"'Finally, I bring from my own heart, the origin of the ministering wind. Gather these things with fire and spirit. Then when the spirit has been restored, when *Archandara, Photaza, Zabythix,* let the doors be thrown open. Let your child come out from the depths and take her place among those who are whole.'"

A breeze that couldn't have come from anywhere lifted the page. It stood straight up for a moment and then fell back onto the book. Then all the other pages followed in succession until the red leather cover slowly closed.

It was done.

Nineteen

The silence was so complete that even the clock stopped ticking. Tasman took a step back from the book. His head hung down. His shoulders raised and lowered as he tried to breathe his way back into his body. Finally he raised his head and blinked. He glanced sheepishly at Val like he was hoping to be praised. Or at least thanked.

The Captain stood up. He carefully carried the book to the cabinet. The door banged shut. He locked it with the key.

Tasman and Val just stood there, not knowing what to do next.

"Tarnation," the Captain shouted. "I let you look, didn't I? Get out of here before I cast a spell on you!"

Val left the shop. She stood by the wedjat and looked at the piece of paper in her hand. Her writing looked strange, especially in the light of day. She could read the words, but they didn't seem like any she would ever write.

Tasman came out and looked over her shoulder. "Did you get it all?"

"I guess. But I don't know what any of it means."

"Wasn't I speaking English? Was it sufficiently Americanized?"

She pointed to the words *Archandara, Photaza,* and *Zabythix.*

"There is no translation for them," Tasman said.

She felt foolish. They'd gone to all this trouble, but she still had no idea what she was supposed to do to help Lanora. She sighed.

"What's the matter?" Tasman said.

"Where am I supposed to find a 'gift from the gods'? Which gods? I don't think we've got the same gods anymore."

"That's what you're supposed to figure out."

"How?"

"You want an instruction manual? A recipe? A scientific formula?"

"Yes."

"That shows a great lack of imagination."

"Since you're imagining this whole thing, why can't you imagine something more specific?"

"Believe me, if I were, I would imagine it differently."

He rolled up the piece of paper and handed it to her. He stuck his hand in his pocket and pulled out a rock, a feather, and three baby teeth. "Alas, I possess no means of securing the scroll. Nothing worthy of this momentous moment, which, for some reason, you have decided to dismiss."

She tightened the tube. "I don't dismiss it. I just worry that it won't help."

"I could share my imagination with you. We could have a meeting of the minds and cause storms with our brains. We could return to the rock and the hard place."

"I guess. But I have to get home now." Val waved.

"Wait." He pulled a thread from a ripped place in his jeans and tied the scroll with that. "It'll be your fault if I become unraveled."

"I think you already are."

Tasman frowned and quickly walked back into the shop.

"Your jeans, I mean," Val called after him.

He didn't answer. She didn't know why he was so sensitive. She stared for a moment at the scroll. Then she went home.

Drew was waiting for her in the hallway outside the apartment door.

"You're in big trouble. Don't even go in there. Run. Run

away. Take this so you won't be hungry. At least not for the first few days." He handed her a large bag of uncooked pasta.

"What's this for?"

"It's all I could reach. I grabbed it when Mom was in the bathroom. Now, go."

He looked so serious that she wanted to laugh and cry.

"They're not *that* mad, are they?"

"Mom said you were something awful. I never heard the word before. It started with a T. She got a phone message. She said you were marked."

"Marked? How?"

"Go!" He pushed her toward the elevator. "Don't take the stairs. They can throw a net down over the railing and catch you."

Val hugged him and opened the front door. "I'm hungry. Can I run away after dinner?"

"But Val, I think they might yell at you."

He was correct.

Mom's face was nothing but straight lines. The pot on the stove was rattling like crazy, on the verge of boiling over.

"Hi, Mom," Val said.

"Mom, I need Val to help me in my room with my homework. Okay? Come on, Val." Drew grabbed Val around the waist.

Mom silently separated Drew from Val, turned down the stove, and pointed to a kitchen chair.

Val sat.

"Your school called," Mom said.

Then Val knew. She had forgotten that they take attendance after lunch. When she hadn't returned, she had been marked truant. "I'm sorry, Mom."

"She's sorry, Mom!" Drew shouted from the safety of the living room.

"Do you know how worried we were?" Mom said.

"My watch stopped during lunch," Val said.

Mom frowned. She vigorously stirred something in a pot on the stove. Red drops splattered all over the jars of dried beans and whole grains that stood guard along the back of the counter. "Don't lie to me."

Val knew she couldn't. But she didn't think her mom would believe the truth. She glanced down at the scroll, which was still in her hand. She slowly hid it behind her leg, hoping her mom wouldn't see it. "Okay, it didn't stop. I lost track of time."

That part was true. Time had disappeared while Tasman read from *The Book of Dares*.

"What were you doing?" Mom accused her.

"I was in a bookstore. Reading." This also was true.

"Reading?"

Val smiled. Reading was the one activity her mom would always approve of.

"What were you reading?"

Val had to think for a moment. She knew she'd better not mention the name of the book. "Something about ancient gods. And goddesses. I'm sorry you were worried, Mom."

Mom sighed and put down the spoon. "I *was* worried. When the school called to say you were missing, I jumped to the conclusion. You see, I know you were in the store when Lanora got in trouble. And I thought, well, maybe you . . ."

"You thought I was shoplifting?" Val couldn't believe it.

"Of course it's unlikely. But it's unlikely that Lanora would. She used to be such a wonderful girl. So clever. So imaginative."

"Maybe she still is."

"Maybe so."

Drew stuck his head into the kitchen. "Are you done being mad at Val because I need her."

"If you really do have homework, then you have to do it yourself," Mom said.

"I need help tying my strings. I don't want my ankle wings to fall off while I'm speeding through the air." He jumped into the kitchen, balancing a feathered object on top of each of his sneakers.

Val picked up one of the squares of denim. Black and white feathers had been glued to one side. The laces were tangled red velvet ribbons. Lanora had made these for Drew several years ago. Val couldn't remember why. "What are they for?"

"Did Werd zap your memory? Is that why you didn't come home? You forgot where you lived and everything from your past?"

"Not everything. I just can't remember why Lanora gave these to you."

"They came from Mercury."

"The planet?"

Drew snorted with disgust. "The messenger to the gods. To give me superfast running powers. I got out my ankle wings so I could warn you that you were in trouble."

"I'm not in trouble anymore."

"You might be again. Tie them on me. Hurry up."

Val picked up the second ankle wing. The black feathers were iridescent. She seemed to hear Tasman's voice whisper, "First, I restore to you a gift from the gods, that my message to you may travel with all possible speed."

She moved her arm so that the feathers flew through the air.

"Give them back." Drew grabbed the feathers and took them into his room.

"Can I borrow them? Just for a little while. It's really important."

Val heard him slam the door. She had to find a way to get Mercury's ankle wings. This couldn't be a coincidence. This had to mean that *The Book of Dares* possessed wisdom after all.

Twenty

Mau trotted along the sidewalk with her tail held high. She wanted to keep well ahead of the man who ran after her shouting, "Vermin!" Mau never acknowledged human speech, except for certain words pertaining to food. She certainly wasn't going to respond to this person. He was far too excited.

In truth, she didn't trust humans. Not even humans she knew. In fact, she trusted them least of all. They often forgot the rule that banned any touching that hadn't been initiated by Mau.

When she reached the street next to the park, she ducked under a parked car to wait for the man to pass. His odor was unusual. But to Mau, he smelled human. The others, with their scents of fake flowers and spices, were the ones who reeked.

"Where'd you go? Can't you get rid of my vermin?" he whimpered.

No, Mau could not.

After the man had staggered on by, she jumped onto the wall and down into the park. She was near the Bower, but she didn't expect to see the girls. They hunted elsewhere now.

She made no sound. She kept herself low to the ground, her tail straight back, her legs slightly bent. She stalked.

She always felt happy in times like these. Her senses alert. Her purpose complete. Anticipation was such a delight; she might never have wanted to actually pounce at anything.

And yet she was hungry. She hadn't had anything to eat since yesterday. Today the offerings of the cat ladies had all been half-eaten, contaminated by some other creature's saliva.

Her nostrils flared. Her whiskers twitched. A mouse would be nice. A squirrel was more of a challenge. A bird wasn't worth the trouble; Mau didn't care much for feathers. She went deeper into the bushes, so deep that she emerged on the other side.

The boy—Tasman—was there.

He sat on a low rock, with his back to her. His hat was on the ground next to him. Mau wasn't pleased. She didn't want to go to her other hunting ground. She was hungry now. She batted his back with her paw.

Tasman turned quickly and then sighed with relief. "Oh. It's you."

Mau flicked her tail back and forth. Whom did he expect? The Bower was her place. The girls were just visitors. Mau hadn't decided if she would allow Tasman to stay.

"Have you seen Val?"

Mau blinked.

"I thought we were meeting here this afternoon. Of course it wouldn't be the first time that what I thought was completely different from what someone else thought. Reality is just a perception. That must be true even for cats."

Mau ignored him and sniffed the air. Was that mouse?

"And yet some people perceive a reality that is much more . . . unreal. Why is that?"

Mau shut her eyes. Not a mouse. It was a dog passing by. A small dog, but still, a dog.

He sighed. "I should have left an hour ago. She makes me dare. Here I am, after all. In the park. And yesterday, I actually read from *The Book of Dares*. Could that be why I came here? Why I risk an encounter with that which cannot be named? Even though I haven't found the incantation bowl. Even though the Captain may have gotten rid of it. Here I sit. Somewhat calmly."

He studied his hands, waiting to see if they would tremble.

"Has a spell been cast on me? I don't care. I do care. I stand on the fence, caught between hope and fear."

He got up and extended his arms, as if he were balancing

on a great precipice, even though his feet were flat on the hard schist.

Mau glared at him. She didn't appreciate sudden movements.

"Tell me what to do, oh wise one. Can my wild nature be cooled down, as you were by the waters of the Nile? Will I be transformed into a gentle cat and settle in the house, as many of your sisters did? Or will I remain like you? The feral cat that walks alone."

Mau blinked several times, as if considering the question.

"I ask you, descendant of the Egyptian goddess Bastet. Killer of rats. Protector of the golden grain. Bastet, what should I do?"

Before she could answer, another human shouted, "Bastet! Bastet!"

It was the man who smelled like human. He reached over the wall to point a pink wand at Mau. "Kill my vermin!"

Mau puffed up her fur until she was three times her typical size. Her ears flattened against her skull. Her head became just a large mouthful of needle-sharp teeth. She hissed and spat as the man climbed over the wall and tumbled to the ground.

Mau hissed and raised her paw to swipe at him.

"You think I'm scared of you? Not after what I see."

Mau growled from deep within her body.

He spent several minutes straightening his sheets and retying the electric cord around his waist. When he had finished, he looked around, shading his eyes with his hand. "What happened to the boy?"

He used the wand to part the bushes. "Boy? Where are you? Who are you, why are you, when are you, what are you?"

Suddenly a blue boot fell to the ground, quickly followed by its mate.

The man picked them up. He sniffed them. He toyed with the buckles. He scratched a few bits of mud from the soles. Finally he looked up to the sky from whence the boots had come. "I need gold," he wailed.

There was no answer.

The man mumbled as he tucked the boots into a large bag. "Nobody gives you what you need. You tell them and tell them. And they throw their junk at you." He shuffled off deeper into the park.

Mau looked up at the tree. Its leaves quivered. Mau sat beneath it. She spent a long time grooming herself to restore order to her fur. Even after the bath was complete, Tasman still hadn't come down.

Twenty-one

When her mom came home from work, Lanora was lying on the sofa. She thought she had time to reach the safety of her bedroom. But her mom was quicker than she used to be. Or maybe Lanora was slower. Whatever the reason, she got caught standing by the TV. Suspended. Dangling between what had happened and what might happen, neither here nor there nor anywhere, really.

"My goodness, are you still in your pajamas?" Emma said.

Lanora looked down, as if surprised to see her sweatpants and her cat T-shirt.

"Didn't you go to school?" Emma said.

Lanora shook her head.

"It isn't going to get any easier," Emma said.

Lanora shut her eyes. She knew that. Each day that passed, each day she was discussed, she became more and more of a freak, and less and less of a Lanora.

"Sweetheart, you have to go to school. Aren't you in enough trouble?"

The word made Lanora wince, as if she felt the broom against her head again, even though it had been an entire day since that miscalculation. The broom had been new. Its bristles soft and still wrapped in plastic. The key had dropped to the sidewalk as Lanora ran down the street. No one bothered to pick it up.

"When I left this morning, you were all dressed. You were going to go. You told me you were going. You promised me."

"I know," Lanora said.

"So what happened?"

What happened? Lanora asked herself this all the time. What had happened?

"Never mind. You'll go tomorrow. Oh. Tomorrow is Saturday. You'll go on Monday. I'll fix us some dinner. How about some macaroni and cheese? You'd like that, wouldn't you?"

Lanora sighed. She didn't like it. Not anymore. The blue boxes with the orange noodle smiles were relics of her past. In fact, the box her mom got out of the cupboard had probably been bought when Lanora was nine years old. When she had eaten so much of the stuff that she'd built a fortress of the empty cartons. NO DADS ALLOWED. When she kept him out so she wouldn't notice he wasn't trying to come in.

"Or maybe we should go to the diner on the corner? You haven't been out all day."

"Yes, I have." Lanora had sat on the fire escape. She had hoped she might find Mau. Even if Mau wouldn't let Lanora hold her, at least Mau would see her for who she had been. But Mau hadn't come to the alley.

"Where did you go?" Emma said.

"Nowhere," Lanora said.

"You didn't go to a store, did you?"

"Of course not."

"So if you didn't go to a store, then why won't you tell me?"

The phone rang. Emma held the receiver out to Lanora.

Lanora walked into the bathroom and shut the door. She turned on the faucet and flushed the toilet and turned on the shower. But she could still hear her mom.

"She doesn't want to talk to you. . . . I don't see how I can make her. . . . No, she didn't go to school. . . . I don't see how I can make her do that, either. . . . I do tell her to go. . . . Fine. You want to threaten her, then come over here and tell her that yourself. . . . No, I haven't set up the community service with Val's mom. . . . You can call her. . . . Because I'm busy. I just got home. I may not be a financial wizard or whatever you call yourself now, but I work, too!"

After a few minutes, her mom tapped on the bathroom door. "Sweetie? If you don't want macaroni, I could make grilled cheese. Or soup? I know, what about we order Chinese? What's that dish you always liked? With the tiny ears of corn. You always said that elves ate them. You tried to keep them, but of course they got all rotten after a few days. Only these wouldn't be rotten. These would be good. Would you like that?"

"No, thank you," Lanora said as politely as she could.

She couldn't be tempted by food, for humans or for elves. All she wanted was to regain control of her life. She wanted to be back on that glorious black stallion with a white blaze on his head, urging him to leap over the obstacles.

The ringing phone sounded very loud at eight o'clock. Drew ran to answer it, even though he had only one arm inside his Superman pajamas. He waved the ringing object over his head. "Mom, it says 'private caller.' But I know who it is, so can I answer?"

"No," Mom said.

"It's got to be Werd. Nobody else is sneaky like that. He probably wants my ankle wings. But he can't have them, either."

Mom took the phone from Drew. "You go on to bed. Your dad will help you."

"Come on, Superman." Dad lifted Drew up to help him fly.

"I'm not Superman. I'm just borrowing his clothes while mine are in the wash," Drew said.

"Hello?" Mom said. "Why, hello, Tom."

Val crept down from her loft bed. Tom was Lanora's dad. He had never called them, not even when Lanora was over at their house and needed to be walked home. Val put her ear against the door to listen. She couldn't hear what Tom was saying, just the footsteps as her mom paced back and forth, saying, "Uh-huh."

Then her mom said, "Of course I'll help Lanora find someplace to do community service. . . . She hasn't? Well, that is serious."

What was serious? Had Lanora's father found out about the hardware store?

Her mom's pacing got faster. Clearly she didn't like what he was saying. "No, I can't make that kind of recommendation. And I don't think that's the answer. . . . Let's hope it won't have to come to that."

Come to what? Val opened her eyes wider as if she could see the words she wasn't able to hear.

"Good night."

Mom hung up.

"What did Tom say?" Dad said softly.

The whispers of her parents were usually as soothing as the wind teasing the leaves of a tree. This time the sound was ominous.

"Lanora stopped going to school," Mom said.

"Why?" Dad said.

"She probably can't face the kids."

"Val would stand by her."

Mom sighed. "I don't think the girls are friends anymore."

Val shut her eyes. It was true, but she didn't like hearing her mom say it.

"So what are they going to do?" Dad said.

"Tom wants to put her in an academy."

"You mean a reform school?"

"They don't call them that anymore."

"But that's what they are. Places to re-form kids."

Val had to put her hand over her mouth to keep from shouting "no!"

There seemed to be only one thing to do. She couldn't wait any longer for Drew to change his mind about giving her the ankle wings. She just had to take them.

She tore a piece of paper from her history notebook and wrote a note.

Dear Drew, I'm a bird and I took my feathers back.

It was lame. Lanora would have invented a better story for why the ankle wings were gone. But Val couldn't ask her. Or Tasman. The best Val could do was add some chicken scratches. She dabbed a little Wite-Out to make a blob of bird poop on the bottom. Then she waited for the apartment to be quiet.

Her parents were watching TV. Val knew they were worried; they weren't talking back to the news. Eventually Mom and Dad left the living room and went into their bedroom.

Val waited. And waited. A clock ticked. Someone screamed on the TV in the apartment next door. A dog barked. A distant siren faded into the night. Finally there was snoring.

Val climbed down from her bed and began her long journey to her brother's room. The apartment wasn't dark. Streetlights and neon signs caused a pale haze in what should have been the night sky. The shapes of the furniture looked like sleeping animals. Val reminded herself that they were friendly creatures as she tiptoed around the sofa, past the rickety table, the tall bookcase, the wide bookcase, and the door to her parents' room.

"Sa-sa-sa-sa-sphew." Her dad spluttered like a cartoon character. She smiled. Only her dad could be funny even in his sleep. Then she continued on.

Drew's room was just past the bathroom.

A great *whoosh* of water made her freeze. But it was someone in the apartment above flushing his toilet.

She pushed the door. His Jupiter nightlight glowed. She tiptoed to a row of hooks where he hung his masks and hats and superhero belts. How would she ever find the ankle wings in that tangle? She patted the objects, hoping to feel the feathers. A metal belt buckle jangled. She glanced at the bed to see if the sound woke him up.

She was in luck. He had gone to sleep clutching the ankle wings in his fist. Now that he was dreaming, his hand dangled off the edge of the mattress.

She knelt down below the bed and touched one red ribbon. She pulled ever so gently. She watched the feathers slip out of his hand.

Suddenly she felt a gun pointed at the side of her head.

A deep voice, or at least as deep as her brother could make his typical squeak, said, "Drop it."

Twenty-two

Court was convened Saturday morning—before breakfast. Val, Drew, and their parents sat at the table. There would be no dancing cereal boxes, no puns about jam, no toast towers to topple. There would just be a serious discussion.

"You do realize that attempted murder is a much worse crime than borrowing," Val said.

"Attempted murder?" Dad said.

"With a marshmallow?" Mom said.

"The gun was pointed at my head," Val said.

"Stealing is stealing," Drew said.

"I didn't actually steal it," Val said.

"Only because, like all superheroes, I sleep with my eyes open and my gun ready," Drew said.

"So you didn't actually shoot me and I didn't actually steal anything. So we're even." Val sneaked a glance at her watch. If this discussion took much longer, she'd be late for soccer.

"That isn't what concerns us," Dad said.

Her parents were looking at her. They weren't paying any attention to Drew. Val had to stick her hands in her armpits to keep from wiping the grin off his face.

"We know some kids get a kind of thrill from bad behavior," Mom said.

Then it hit Val. This was going to be about Lanora. "I'm not like that."

"We know that you aren't. But . . ."

Val winced when she heard the "but." Parents could always stick one in. No matter what was being discussed. No matter how well you argued. No matter if you were right and they agreed. They could turn it all upside down. Yes, of course we know that you're older now and should be allowed to walk by yourself, *but* not after dark. And not anyplace fun.

"I'm never going to be like that," Val insisted.

"I would agree. But I would never have thought you'd steal from your brother."

"I wasn't stealing."

"When you take something without permission, it's stealing," Dad said.

"And you did *not* have my permission. You had the opposite of my permission. You had my . . ." Drew paused while he worked it out in his head. Finally he shouted triumphantly, "Noise-sim-rep!"

"We're very concerned that you thought you could take whatever you wanted without considering anyone else's feelings."

"But I wasn't being selfish. I was thinking about Lanora."

"What does this have to do with Lanora?" Mom said.

"Nothing," Val said.

"Then why did you bring her up?" Mom said.

"Never mind. You wouldn't understand." Val slumped into her chair.

These were the wrong words to say to Mom. She prided herself on her ability to walk a mile in anyone's shoes—except those women who wore superhigh heels.

"I might. Believe me, adults are just as susceptible to peer pressure as kids. Didn't I go see that movie that I knew I would hate just because everybody else was going?"

"You didn't hate it as much as you thought you would," Dad said.

"I hated it enough," Mom said.

Val started to relax. Her parents were squabbling about their typical adult stuff. Maybe it would be okay. Maybe she could still get to soccer before the captain made the latecomers do extra pushups.

"What movie was it?" Val said.

"You know, the one about the superhero?" Mom said.

"Drew should have gone." Val smiled at Drew. He could talk about his favorite topic all day.

She had underestimated her little brother. He pointed his finger at her. "Don't let her change the subject. She hasn't been punished yet."

"That's right," Dad said.

"Okay. So what's my punishment?" Val decided it would save time to plead guilty.

"Community service," Mom said.

"You mean, clean my room?" Val said.

"No. Soup kitchen. You can come with me today."

"But I have soccer. I can't let down my team," Val said.

"You should have remembered them last night," Dad said.

"Can't I do a different community service after practice?" Val said.

"No. I want you to pay attention to people who have less than you do. Then maybe you'll appreciate what you have," Mom said.

The soup kitchen was in a church. Mom led Val past the ornate front entrance guarded by stone gargoyles, around the corner to the back. A line of people waited. New York was full of lines. Lines for movies, for plays, for tables at restaurants, for special milk shakes, for fancy dancing clubs. Some New Yorkers joined a line whenever they saw one just in case it led to something exciting. This wasn't that kind of line.

The people waited patiently. They weren't chatting, checking phones, reading, amusing themselves. They were just waiting. For soup.

Val wanted to say to her mom, Okay, I get it now. She used to feel this way in math class, when the teacher went on and on about the least common denominator. Val always wanted to tell him he could stop talking about those slices of pizza. She knew who got what share. Of course these people hadn't gotten any shares. They stood, waiting, for whatever they could get.

Val's mom greeted many of them by name. She asked people about their arthritis, complimented a brightly colored shirt, joked about the weather.

One man wore a pale blue toga. His hair was a nest of snakes. He waved a pink wand around his head.

"Watch what you're doing. You'll poke my eye out," someone said.

"Can't you be still?" someone else said.

"Got to keep them away. Away, away, away, away." The man made a full circle.

Val's mom rushed toward the man and put her hand on

the wand. The man stopped spinning. "This seems quite powerful. I think you'd better keep it in your belt for now," Mom said.

The man shook it at her. "If it's powerful, then why are the vermin eating all the gold?"

He looked at Val. It was the man she had seen in the park. She took a step back behind her mom. The man peered at her. "You tell me why."

"Me? I don't know," Val said.

"We'll be opening the door soon. You can have some lunch," Val's mom said.

The man left the line and wandered down the street, waving his wand in a big circle around his head. "Don't want lunch. Want gold! Need gold. Got-got-got get-get-get go-go-gold!"

Twenty-three

A man dropped a wooden crate on the floor. The crash woke Mau.

"Watch what you're doing there. Can't you read?" the Captain shouted.

The word "fragile" had been written on the crate in three languages. None of them were English.

After the man left, Mau hopped down from the windowsill and trotted over to the crate. She sniffed. Yes, she could tell there had been mice. She licked her lips.

"Tasman! Got something new here!" the Captain called.

There was no answer.

"Where is he hiding?" the Captain said to Mau. "Tasman! Get over here! Bring your notebook. There's work to be done."

From the far corner of the shop, footsteps shuffled closer and closer. Tasman appeared. If possible, his hair was wilder than usual. His eyes were puffy. He wore old slippers on his feet. He held up his notebook and a pen, but he didn't speak.

"Were you sleeping?" the Captain said.

Tasman shook his head.

"Are you sick?" the Captain said.

Tasman shook his head.

"Then what's the matter with you?" the Captain said.

Tasman just stared at the Captain.

"Bah." The Captain got a long knife from his workbench and approached the crate. He used the tip of the knife to pry loose metal staples from the top.

"Stand back till I see what we got. Last shipment I got from Alexandria was full of poisonous spiders."

"I'm not afraid of spiders," Tasman said.

"You never got bit by one. That's your trouble. You're afraid of the wrong things." The Captain used the knife as a lever to lift up the lid.

Mau crouched, ready to pounce at whatever came out. Nothing did. The box seemed to be full of crumpled newspaper. The Captain speared some with his knife and flung them onto the floor.

"Then there was the time I got a snake. Of course it was dead. I never did find out if it was alive when the journey started."

The Captain pushed aside more paper until he uncovered something wrapped in cloth. "Ah, now *this* will be interesting." He put down the knife and put on his grimy white gloves. Gently, oh so gently, he lifted the swaddled object from its nest of papers and placed it on his desk.

"It looks like a baby," Tasman whispered.

"I hope not. Don't need anybody sending me another kid."

Tasman looked at his slippers and said nothing.

"Stop standing around like a landlubber. Make yourself useful. Cut the twine."

Tasman picked up the knife and carefully sawed through the strands.

The Captain unwrapped the cloth. A bit of brown could be seen.

Tasman leaned closer. "Is it another bowl?"

It was a brown stone box.

Tasman sat on a stack of books.

"Limestone." The Captain slowly lifted up the lid and placed it on his desk. Inside there were seven objects made of white alabaster. "Ah. Ceremonial objects. Haven't seen any like these since that time we opened up the tomb near Luxor."

Two were small bottles. Four were small cups. The Captain picked up the central piece—a long tube that divided into two curves at one end. He brought the tip of the tube closer to Tasman's face. "The priests used this for the ritual of the Opening of the Mouth."

Tasman shrank away from it.

The Captain laughed. "Don't be scared. It's not for making people talk. Wish it was." He waved the tube in front of Tasman again. "Never thought I'd be saying you were too quiet."

"So what is it for?" Tasman said.

"If you touch this to the mouth of a dead person, then he can breathe and drink. The little cups are to offer the poor fellow something. He'll be thirsty after you bring him back. The Egyptians put different things in the bottles. You had a choice of milk, salt water, or fresh water. Of course, if it were me, I'd be wanting something else."

Mau came over to sniff the smallest cup.

"Get away from there, you mangy beast." The Captain waved his arm at Mau. She didn't move. She glared at the Captain.

"Look at the both of you, staring at me." The Captain pointed the tube at Tasman again. "Come on. Tell me what you want. Is it new boots?"

Tasman tucked his feet underneath him. "I don't need new boots."

"What happened to your other ones anyway?"

"I lost them. Because you wouldn't let me have the bowl," Tasman said.

The Captain pounded his fist against the side of a shelf.

Dishes jumped. A small candlestick toppled over. Mau darted away.

"How many times do I have to tell you? I don't have the incantation bowl."

"How could you sell it? Didn't you know I'd need it?" Tasman said.

"Bah," the Captain said. "Don't you need the money more? Don't you need to eat? Have a roof over your head?"

Tasman picked at a tear in his slipper. "Those aren't the only things that matter."

"Then you tell me what does. You tell me why you want that bowl." The Captain filled a glass with wine.

"Then you do have it? You didn't sell it?"

The Captain held up his hand. "Didn't say that. Don't be twisting my words. I just asked why."

"Why is the sky blue? Why does a baby smile? Why do some people have too much imagination and other people not nearly enough?"

The Captain drank from the glass. "You read too many books. You know that?"

"They're your books."

"I know. But I don't read them. I just sell them."

"Like the bowl," Tasman said.

"That's right. Like the bowl. Now, quit daydreaming and write up that crap we got today." The Captain stood up and walked toward the back room.

As he passed a stack of boxes, he paused. He placed his hand against the second box. It was completely wrapped in tape. He looked back over his shoulder at Tasman.

"Don't you want new boots?" he said.

"Why? I'm never going out again," Tasman said.

"Tarnation," the Captain said. He pounded his fist against the box. The stack leaned precariously. Tasman jumped up and raced over to help the Captain keep the boxes from falling.

When he placed his hand on the second box, he stared at the Captain. "What's in here, anyway?"

"I don't know. What's the label say? Alabaster canopic jars."

"That's not your writing," Tasman said.

"Bah." The Captain straightened the stack. "What do you know about it? Nothing. Now get to work."

But Tasman had recognized the scrawl. It was his grandfather's.

Twenty-four

On Monday morning, Drew tied on Mercury's ankle wings with triple knots. He kicked his legs up in Val's face to show her.

"You shouldn't wear pieces of dead animals to school. You'll upset the other kids," Val said.

"They aren't pieces of dead animals. Live birds voluntarily gave Lanora their feathers," Drew said.

Val knew she could never win an argument with her brother. She had to figure out another way to persuade him to give her what she needed to help Lanora. So Val skipped soccer practice to get Drew from his after-school program.

He wasn't glad to see her. "You're too late. During lunchtime, I permanently attached Mercury's ankle wings to my legs." He danced and dashed ahead, as if he were a messenger for the gods. To his disappointment, no one noticed him. This was New York City, where even movie star gods and goddesses didn't receive more than a ripple of attention from the vast human sea.

A stoplight made him wait at the corner. Val caught up with him. "I have money for ice cream."

"Why would I trade a superpower for something that melts?"

"Because ice cream is real."

"So are these." Drew danced again. "Besides, there's ice cream at home."

"Old boring vanilla with ice crystals," Val said.

"I love ice crystals. Crystals are another source of power."

"Hmm," Val said. That was what she needed. Something more powerful than Drew's imagination. She knew of only one thing. She took her brother's hand and turned him to the right.

"Why aren't we going to the park?" Drew said.

"Why should I do what you want when you won't do what I want?" Val said.

"Because what I want is fun and what you want is dumb," Drew said.

"We're going someplace much better than the park," Val said.

They headed west along 86th Street and crossed Amsterdam Avenue.

"Are we going to the other park?" Drew said.

"You'll see," Val said.

He paused to tighten the laces of the ankle wings. She didn't wait. He had to run to catch up.

"I don't think you know where you're going. I think you are leading me astray. After we walk in circles for an hour, you think I'll be tired and you can overpower me."

"Nope," Val said.

"I warn you that I have hidden supplies of energy. Three people had birthdays today so I am full of cupcakes."

"I'm not trying to make you tired."

"Then where are we going?"

"You'll see." She was taking him the long way around to build suspense. They walked three more blocks, the last two because she got a little lost for real.

Then there was the sign. ANTIQUITIES FROM THE SHIP-WRECK OF TIME

"Wow, look at that." Drew ran ahead, but he waited for Val to come before he dared to go in the yard. The wedjat seemed to wink at them. A large crow croaked a warning as it flew away from the upstairs railing. The setting was perfect for persuading Drew—except for one thing. The rusty gate was chained shut. A piece of paper was stuck to a nail. GONE FISHING

Val rattled the chain. No one came to the gate. Not even Mau.

Drew pressed his nose against the grimy window.

"Wow," he said again when he saw the statue with the chiseled nose.

"How could the Captain go fishing? There's no place to fish around here," Val said.

"Actually the Hudson River has excellent fishing, unless you plan on feeding what you catch to a pregnant woman."

A pair of feet wearing tattered slippers stuck out from behind the trash can labeled RECYCLED PAPER. Val didn't recognize them until she saw the frayed part of his jeans.

"What are you doing out here?" Val said.

"The Captain locked me out." Tasman jumped up and stood in such a way so that she couldn't stare at his feet.

"Why?" Val said.

"He didn't appreciate the way I unpacked some of his boxes."

"Did you find it?" Val said.

"I'm getting closer," Tasman said.

"That's great," Val said.

"Yes. Except it meant he didn't want me in the store while he went fishing."

"Is he really fishing?" Drew said.

"No. That's his way of saying that he is in search of treasure," Tasman said.

"Buried?" Drew said.

"If by buried you mean in the dirt, then no, but if by buried you mean hidden to the unobservant, then yes."

"Who *are* you?" Drew said.

Val thought Tasman would answer that question with a speech about the composition of his cells and what he had for breakfast. But Tasman just said, "A friend of your sister's."

"Did you know she is a thief?" Drew said.

"Val?" Tasman looked at Val with new respect.

"She snuck into my bedroom in the middle of the night to steal Mercury's ankle wings." Drew pointed to his legs.

Tasman's eyes widened. Then he smiled at Val.

She was glad he understood why she had brought Drew here.

"That's terrible. How did you stop her?" Tasman said.

"With my gun. I would have shot her, too. Except that she is my sister. And she likes marshmallows."

"I'm glad you showed restraint. It would have been a shame to waste the marshmallows on her," Tasman said.

"Have you been in that store?" Drew said.

"Many times. I even sleep there. If a person can sleep in the presence of millions of eyes."

"Watching you?" Drew said.

"Leading words like 'imagination,' 'insubordination,' 'incantation.'"

Drew thought that was hysterical. "What grade are you in?"

"I think, at the present time, I'm in 1st, 8th, 10th, 5th, 9th, and 17th."

"I mean, at school," Drew said.

"As I said: 1st, 8th, 10th, 5th, 9th, and 17th are the levels I've achieved in my various studies. In case you're wondering, I'm only in 1st grade at following directions."

"You don't go to school?" Drew said.

"If by 'go' you mean actually set foot in a brick-and-mortar structure, then no, I don't."

Drew considered this for a moment. "Either you are very smart. Or very dumb."

Tasman laughed. "I fear that I am the latter. But *you* are very smart." Tasman pointed at Drew. "That's why you arranged this meeting."

"I did?" Drew said.

"Of course. You know why Val wants Mercury's ankle wings. You're all in favor of that noble cause. But you thwarted her to make sure she brought you here to join our crusade."

Val shook her head vigorously at Tasman. How dare he invite Drew in? He obviously didn't have a little brother.

"Right." Drew stood up as tall as he could.

"You swear to support our crusade, and to not tell

parents, and to eschew personal possessions?" Tasman said, raising his right hand.

Val smiled. No way would Drew know that "eschew" meant "give up."

"Yes. Except Mercury's ankle wings," Drew said.

"Come on, Drew." Val kicked a rock. It clattered against the trash can.

"They're mine. Lanora made them for me. And she won't be making me anything else because Val got Lanora mad at her and she never comes over."

"I didn't get her mad at me." Val stepped menacingly toward Drew.

Tasman stood between them. He put his hands on Drew's shoulders. "It's because of Lanora that we need Mercury's ankle wings."

"You mean she really is under a spell?" Drew whispered.

Tasman nodded solemnly.

"Poor Lanora," Drew said.

"So you see why we need to help her," Val said.

Drew squatted down so he could stroke the feathers. "Will I get them back?"

"Yes," Val said.

Tasman shook his head. "We can't promise. We don't know what will happen. But if you let me have them, you might get Lanora back."

"How? What are you going to do with them?" Drew said.

Tasman whispered loudly in his ear. "The mysteries have yet to be revealed."

"Then how do you know what to do?" Drew whispered.

Tasman pointed to the wedjat.

It slowly swung back and forth, even though none of them could feel a breeze.

Drew frowned and stroked his chin as if he had a beard. Finally he said, "Okay."

Val immediately started untying the ankle wings before he could reconsider.

"Wait!" Drew slapped her hands away.

Val hadn't expected him to change his mind so soon.

Tasman put one hand on Drew's wrist and the other on Val's. "Drew's right. The transfer is important. It requires a special ceremony."

"At the Bower," Drew said.

"At the Bower?" Neither Tasman nor Val wanted to go there.

But Drew danced away from the shop and along the sidewalk. "At the Bower."

Lanora never went to the park. Too many kids hung out there. She had to avoid kids. The ones in middle school might have recognized her. And it would have been painful to see the younger ones. The ones in their princess costumes. The ones who still believed in happy-ever-afters. The ones who still had a chance. The ones who hadn't yet made the mistake of ignoring their friends and throwing away their good luck charms.

Did Lanora really believe her demise was all because of the lilac butterfly? Of course not. But she did believe there was only one way to stop from wondering if that were true. She had to go back to the Bower and dig it up.

She was just about to climb over the wall to enter the park when she heard a little boy say, "I don't want to give them to Val."

There was no mistaking Drew. Lanora quickly ducked down. She pulled up the hood of her sweatshirt.

"Why not?"

Lanora didn't recognize this voice. It belonged to an older boy.

"Yeah, why not?"

This was Val.

"She doesn't know anything about ceremonies," Drew said.

Lanora smiled. Val didn't. She had to be coached along every step. But that was okay. Val was much better at other things, things that Lanora was terrible at. Things like being loyal. And fearless.

"And so how would you arrange for the transfer of the

object? Considering that we lack sacrificial altars and we really aren't interested in any kind of bloodshed, even if it's metaphorical."

Who was this guy? Why was he there with Val and Drew? How had Val met him? Nobody like that went to M.S. 10.

"Come on, Drew. Tell us what you want to do," Val said.

"Wellllllll," Drew said.

Lanora smiled. She wondered what Drew would come up with. His imagination was pretty intense. She inched along the wall, a little bit closer to where they were.

"I think that Val should kneel down in front of me, press her forehead to the ground three times," Drew said.

"Three times?" Val said.

"Okay. Nine times," Drew said.

"That's more!" Val said.

"And then, *if* the laces come undone, she can be allowed to remove Mercury's ankle wings," Drew said.

Lanora had forgotten all about the ankle wings. They were so old, they had to be falling apart. She could understand why Drew might want to play with things like that. But why would Val bother with them? And why would that guy?

"Are you *sure* you want the spirits to do that? If it were me, I wouldn't want them untying things so close to my skin," the guy said.

"Why not?" Drew said.

"Because of the energy required to move the laces. To overcome gravity and inertia and the power of non-belief."

"What's that?"

"That's what you're thinking. That they won't do it. So they'll have to blast through your brain. Because it will happen. The laces will be untied. And then the ankle wings will fall to the ground and get contaminated."

Lanora smiled in spite of herself. The guy was a master of manipulation. But why was he going to all this trouble?

"Okay. Take them off. No, not you, Val. Tasman should do it," Drew said.

Tasman? What kind of a name was that, Lanora wondered. She had to see what he looked like. It ought to be safe. They were busy with their ceremony. She adjusted her hood. She slowly raised herself up until she could just barely peek over the top of the wall.

Tasman wasn't cute, Lanora decided. Not by any real standard. His hair was too wild. His expressions were unpredictable. His ears were crooked. Although that could have been because of the way he bent over Drew's feet. He seemed clumsy. He couldn't get the laces untied. Val came forward to help. Val always wanted to help. Drew kicked at his sister. Val stepped back. Tasman smiled at Val.

It was a brilliant smile.

It was painful to see.

The knots were undone at last. Tasman lifted the ankle wings up above his head, as if he were making an offering to the sun. The light, dappled by the leaves of the trees, shone upon the black and the white. The feathers stirred to life. Was it the wind? Or did another sort of power animate them?

Lanora wished Tasman would put on the ankle wings. She wanted him to run like the wind to deliver messages from the gods. She wanted him to bring one to her. To tell her that everything would be okay.

Because if all those things happened, then maybe it would be.

Twenty-five

Val did something she never in a million years expected to do. She thanked her little brother. In public. While they were walking home from the park.

He nodded his head to accept her gratitude. "I'm happy to be a hero. It's what I was born to do. But if I won't get the ankle wings back, you should probably give me something else."

Val wondered what that should be. "Maybe a different kind of wings? Like those?" She pointed to a little girl dancing along the sidewalk with fairy wings looped to her shoulders.

"I was thinking cold, hard cash."

Val reached in her pocket and took out a quarter.

Drew shook his head. "Is that all you think they're worth?"

Val sighed. He had her trapped. "Okay. I'll give you more

when we get home. We'd better hurry. I don't want Mom mad at me for being late again."

"Mom and Dad will understand when we tell them," Drew said.

Val grabbed Drew's shoulders. "You can't tell them. Remember you swore not to tell any parents. That includes ours."

"Not even if they get mad?" Drew said.

"Especially if they get mad. Come on. Let's race. Then we won't be late."

They ran the last three blocks, through the lobby, and up the stairs. Drew got to their apartment first. "Ha-ha! I beat you. I told you I was a hero!"

It wasn't a fair contest. Her backpack contained the weight of global history; all he had in his was what he hadn't wanted to eat for lunch.

Mom greeted them at the door. "Dinner's ready."

They took their usual places at the round table in the dining alcove. As she sat down, Val shifted her chair so she could be in kicking range of Drew. Her dad moved it back. Drew grinned.

"You look very pleased with yourself. Did something good happen at school?" Dad said.

"What good thing could possibly happen at school?" Drew said.

"Maybe you learned something interesting?" Mom said.

Drew leaned forward and whispered loudly. "I did. But not at school."

Val glared at Drew.

"So what did you and Val do after she picked you up?" Mom said.

Drew looked at Val. "Nothing."

"Nothing?" Mom was instantly suspicious.

Val couldn't believe her brother couldn't come up with a better lie. "I rescued Drew from prison and we hid from the bloodhounds."

"Let your brother talk," Mom said. "Tell me more about this nothing."

Drew smiled. "Well." He scooped a bite of potatoes onto his fork. He waved it in the air. He pointed it at Val. "Val took me to meet a boy."

"A boy?" Mom leaned forward. "From her school?"

"No. He doesn't go to school," Drew said.

"Is he homeschooled?" Mom said.

"He's smarter than that," Drew said.

"No matter how smart he is, he still needs to go to school." Mom put down her fork and stared at Val.

Val quickly crammed potatoes into her mouth. It would be rude to answer any questions with her mouth full. Unfortunately it didn't take long to chew mashed potatoes.

"How did you meet him?" Mom said.

"At a bookstore," Val said.

"Where does he live?" Mom said.

Val shrugged.

"I know," Drew said.

"You do?" Val said.

"He lives in the store. With all the other things that have been shipwrecked by time. That's why he doesn't go to school. Or even to get a haircut. Because time washed him ashore in a place he didn't mean to be. But that was okay. Except it messed up his clothes."

Val watched her parents both wipe the smiles off their faces with their napkins.

"I bet he has superpowers," Dad said.

"Yes. He has the power to make people change their minds," Drew said.

"I wish I had that power. Then maybe I could get an appointment to see the mayor," Mom said.

"Why do you want to see the mayor?" Val was eager to change the subject.

"Remember I told you how the people at the soup kitchen are losing their permit to prepare food?" Mom explained about her most recent effort to fight City Hall.

After dinner, Val went into Drew's room to deliver what she hoped was an adequate payoff. She opened the map of the United States and dumped her entire collection of state quarters on his bed.

He lifted handfuls of silver. The coins clinked satisfyingly as they dribbled through his fingers. He smiled. "I accept this ransom. But only because I realize how difficult it is to get diamonds these days."

"Oh, thank you, wise lord." Val bowed to him.

Drew sadly shook his head. "You just don't know how to play, do you?"

"What was wrong with that?"

Drew patted her on the shoulder. "That's okay. You have other uses. And you have an interesting friend."

She didn't want to discuss Tasman with Drew. "Good night, Pest."

"Good night, Bossy Pants."

She was at his door when he said, "Do you think the ankle wings broke the spell? Is Lanora saved now?"

"Maybe."

"What do you mean, maybe?" Drew jumped on his bed so he could be as tall as Val. He glared at her.

She was afraid to tell him she had two more things to get. The gift from the Star Tamer. And the gift from her own heart. She hadn't even figured out what those things were. Or what she should do with them when she had all three. What if they weren't enough? What if she also needed the incantation bowl? How could she get something that might not exist?

"I don't want to trade my ankle wings for a maybe!" Drew hissed at her.

"The maybe is . . . I don't know if it happened yet. That's all. Now I have to do my homework."

"That's what you always say."

"Because I always do."

She went back to her room and got out her homework. The books surrounded her on her bed. She opened her history book. She found a map of the world. What country had *The Book of Dares* come from? Did that place even still exist?

She took the scroll of parchment from its hiding place under the mattress. She unrolled it and looked at what she had written. The handwriting was unrecognizable, even though she knew she had been the one to hold the pen.

Second, I bring to you a gift from the Star Tamer, who from his great heights has given proof of his devotion to our cause.

Who was the Star Tamer?

She looked out the window at the night sky. The bright light she thought was a star turned out to belong to a jet. But she could see the moon.

Several blocks of buildings separated her apartment from Lanora's. Val remembered when Lanora had decided that if they both looked at the moon at the same time, their lines of sight would meet on its surface in the Mare Nubium— the Sea of Clouds. Everyone knew the moon reflected the sun's light. But if the moon reflected other things, as well, Lanora and Val could send each other messages—allowing, of course, for the time it took to travel 500,000 miles there and back. This had been an exciting discovery—when they were nine. Val doubted that Lanora was looking at the moon and sending her thought waves now.

It seemed much more possible that Tasman was.

Twenty-six

Each morning, Emma tried different ways to make Lanora get out of bed. She played soothing music. She played military marches. She cooked bacon. She burned the toast. She said, "Rise and shine, sweetheart." But Lanora didn't rise and she certainly didn't shine. She ignored her mom's efforts. She buried under her blankets until she heard her mom screech, "You have to go to school!" Then the door slammed as Emma left for work.

This morning was like every other except for one thing. Lanora had seen the boy with the amazing eyes. The one with Val. Lanora wouldn't refer to him as Val's boyfriend. Even if he was, which Lanora doubted, she didn't have to call him that. His name was Tasman.

Tasman didn't go to school, either. Lanora instinctively knew this by the way his mind traveled way beyond the limitations of a classroom. She wondered what he had done. Had he been suspended? Or bullied? Was he scared?

Or was he brave? Why hadn't he gone back? More importantly, where did *he* go all day? If she met him, would he say, "Are you taking a gap year, too? Are you trying to find yourself?"

Then she would shake her head. "No, I want to lose myself."

And he would get it.

She shut her eyes for a moment. Being understood had seemed an impossible dream—until she had seen Tasman.

She quickly got out of bed and put on her typical disguise of jeans and a gray hoodie. Then she returned to her closet. She needed to wear something else if she wanted him to recognize her as a kindred spirit. Most boys didn't pay attention to clothes. But he would appreciate the sea green gauze shirt her mom had bought for that costume party. Its sleeves ended in triangle points, just below her knees. It had meanings she couldn't begin to guess.

She left the apartment and ran down the three flights of stairs. The sun was shining. The sky was blue. New York City brimmed with possibilities again.

At the Museum of Natural History, gigantic orbs floated inside a great glass building. They were so large and yet they were mere models of the planets. She wished she could hear what he had to say about that. But he wasn't there. Instead, a yellow school bus disgorged a swarm of small children, so she moved on.

Would he go to the park? Would he go back to the Bower? For some reason, he had seemed nervous there. And so she walked in the opposite direction.

Coffee shops? Could he afford to buy something? Maybe not. He had been wearing such awful old slippers.

Where could he go to delight his extraordinary mind? The public library, of course.

She climbed the steps and pushed through the old wooden doors. What would he want to learn about? She avoided the kids' section and walked among the shelves with more challenging books. Science? Philosophy? History? She paused by a row of encyclopedias. She took the volume with the *T*. She wanted to learn why his name sounded familiar even though no one she knew had been called that.

She sat at a table and opened the book. There was a famous Tasman in the 17th century. Abel Tasman was an explorer. Many places had been named after him, including the large island off the coast of Australia. The encyclopedia had a picture of a cartoon monster called the Tasmanian Devil. But it didn't tell her what she wanted to know. How had Abel Tasman found the courage to venture into the unknown? How could he stand on the deck of a small ship and sail on toward an empty sea? Battered by storms, blown off course, confronted by hostile Maoris in New Zealand, he survived it all and made his way back to his world. But he had not been welcomed as a hero. Since he hadn't found anything useful, the Dutch East India Company decided to use a more "persistent explorer" for future expeditions.

In other words, everybody thought he had failed.

That wasn't at all what she hoped to find out.

She pushed away from the book on the table and left the library.

The sidewalks were as crowded as usual. People walked past her. They were in a hurry. They knew where they were going. They were eager to reach their destinations. Nothing was blowing them off course.

Then someone stopped directly in front of her. Lanora's head was down, but she recognized the muddy sneakers.

It was Val.

Lanora looked up, but only briefly. She didn't want to see pity in Val's eyes.

Neither one spoke. Neither one knew what to say. There was too much to say.

Lanora tried the smile, the one she was practicing for when she returned to M.S. 10. But her mouth trembled like a weight lifter whose muscles quavered with exertion. She couldn't hold the pose. The barbells crashed to the floor.

Val decided not to run after Lanora. Sometimes you just had to let your teammate take a time-out on the sidelines. You had to focus on your own playing, if the game was still in progress. Val needed to find the gift from the Star Tamer, whoever he or she was. *Second, I bring to you a gift from the Star Tamer, who from his great heights has given proof of his devotion to our cause.*

Which "heights"? What was "devotion"? What kind of "star"? What kind of "gift"? Val felt like she didn't know anything anymore. She had to be pretty ignorant, really, if she didn't know how to talk to her friend.

Lunchtime was almost over. The members of the Poetry Club had uncharacteristically been outside and were now heading back to school. Helena was leading the way, as usual. Tina was looking at the world from the corner of her eye. Gillian was clomping along in her big boots. Olivia greeted Val first with her beautiful smile. "Look, it's Val."

"With furrowed brow." Today Helena had added one bit of color to her black ensemble. The pop tab had been joined by a red button.

"Expressions should have an expiration date. Nobody furrows anymore." Tina smoothed her bangs to cover up her own forehead.

"Would you accept a corduroy brow?" Gillian said.

"What's a Star Tamer?" Val interrupted their game.

The poets pondered this for only the briefest of seconds.

"An astronomer." As usual, Helena was first with a response.

"A circus performer." Olivia clapped her hands with delight.

"A gossip columnist," Tina said.

Val shook her head. "It must be something else."

"Why do you want to know?" Helena said.

"Context is crucial," Gillian said.

"He lives up in the heights," Val said.

"Washington Heights?" Olivia said.

"Wuthering Heights?" Helena said.

"Please, no more Brontë sisters," Tina said.

"Am I allowed to mention their evil father, who paid hardly any attention to his brilliant daughters?" Helena said.

"No!" the other poets shouted.

But Val said, "Yes," and pumped her fist.

"You figured out who the Star Tamer is?" Helena said.

"Is the answer symbolic?" Gillian said.

"Metaphoric?" Olivia said.

"Acronymic?" Tina said.

Val couldn't tell them it was Lanora's father.

But how would Val find him? She had only met Mr. Nuland three times—four, if you counted the day she and Lanora had seen him steering a woman in high heels to a fancy brunch spot on Columbus Avenue.

"Well, well," Lanora had said, "my father's got an antidote to my mom."

"What's that?" Val had asked.

"A cure."

Val hadn't understood how one person could be a cure for another. She suspected Lanora had gotten the word wrong. Lanora sometimes did. She claimed that was the price you paid for using power words. But now Val knew what Lanora meant. Probably Lanora had hoped the A Team would be an antidote for Val.

After the divorce, Mr. Nuland rarely came to the Upper West Side. He usually sent a car to whisk Lanora across town to what she called an "edifying event."

Val hoped her parents knew where he worked.

After dinner that night, Drew asked her several times if anybody at her school had been saved from a wicked spell that day. When she said there weren't any superheroes at M.S. 10, he threatened to go to her school to get the job done.

He raced around the apartment, collecting the shower curtain, the dustpan, Mom's hairbrush, a spray bottle of window cleaner, a copper colander, and Val's shin guards.

"That's enough. If you really have superpowers, you shouldn't need any more stuff," Mom said.

"Yes, I do. I still need the you-know-what that you-know-who has," Drew hissed at Val.

The clock cuckooed. Luckily it was Drew's bedtime.

"Good night, little brother," Val said.

Drew growled as their parents escorted him into his bedroom.

While they were saying good night to him, Val sat on the sofa with her homework notebook on her lap. She tried to plan what she was going to say. It was hard. She wished she had a soccer ball. Talking to people was easier when she kicked something at them. Could she throw a pillow at her dad and say, "Think fast, where's Mr. Nuland's office?"

Val heard the little tinkle of chimes that somehow had come to represent rain falling on the ground to help dreams blossom.

Dad said, "Good night, Drew."

The door shut and her parents came into the living room.

"Look!" Dad did a double take. "A sixth grade girl is sitting in our living room. Doesn't she realize she should choose to be anyplace in the world where her parents won't be?"

Mom smiled at Val. "Care for a sandwich, sweetie?"

"Yes, please," Val said.

"Ham on rye?" Dad said.

"Then you'd be in the middle," Mom said.

"Ha ha," Dad said.

Her parents sat on either side of her. Val leaned her head back. Not so very long ago, her head used to sink into the soft cushions. But she had grown. Now her head clunked against the hard wall.

"Panini?" Mom said.

Val nodded.

Her parents pressed in tighter. They were warm and solid against her.

"Did you say what kind of sandwich you were?" Dad said.

"Jam," Val said.

"Ah. And why would that be?" Dad said.

Val remembered again how painful it was to be face-to-face with Lanora and have nothing to say. And if Lanora went away, Val would never have the chance to make things right.

"Do people really go to reform school?" Val said.

"You can't send me. I refuse to go," Dad said.

Val sighed.

Mom sighed, too. "Are you worrying about Lanora?"

"Oh, gosh, I'm an idiot," Dad said.

Mom leaned over to pat his knee. Then she squeezed Val's shoulders.

"Adjusting to middle school isn't easy. Lanora will be okay. She just needs the support of a little counseling.

Emma's having trouble with the insurance, but I know that Tom will pay out of pocket."

"He can afford it," Dad said.

"What does he do?" Val tried to sound casual, even though this was exactly what she needed to know.

"He picks up piles of money and moves them to a new place where they can become bigger piles of money." Mom demonstrated with the magazines on the coffee table.

"It's more complicated than that," Dad said.

"Oh, right. I forgot the part where he takes some off the pile each time he moves it." She took one of the magazines and stuck it under her arm.

"But where?" Val said.

"The piles are in things called derivatives. Don't ask me to explain because I can't." Mom raised her hands helplessly.

"No, I mean, where does Mr. Nuland work?"

Twenty-seven

The Internet told Val that Geld Inc. had its offices at 500 Park Avenue. The Internet showed Val which block the building was on, which subway to use to get there, with two alternate routes, and how long it would take. The Internet even warned her that there was a seventy percent chance of an afternoon shower. Yes, the Internet had told Val everything she needed to know except the most important thing. How was she going to get the chance to speak to Mr. Nuland?

When Val came up from the subway tunnel, the streets of Midtown Manhattan glistened with moisture. The top of the building was hidden by the cloud that had so recently shed its rain. The building's glass walls had no cracks or chinks. The only opening was on the ground level. A revolving door was spitting out whatever people had dared to enter.

In this world Mr. Nuland wasn't Lanora's father, he was

chief executive officer. And even if she did get in to see him, what would she say? That Lanora had buried her lilac butterfly at the Bower. That Mau had taken the butterfly to an antiquities shop. That Val had met a strange kid there who read from *The Book of Dares*. And because that passage mentioned a Star Tamer's gift, Val had come to collect it.

Yeah, right.

Tasman might have known something better to say, but he wasn't there. Val was supposed to meet him later on the steps of the Natural History Museum—after she had gotten the gift from the Star Tamer.

Val watched three more people get spit out of the revolving door. She clenched and unclenched her fists. There was always a moment before each soccer game when time stopped. The players were lined up across the field. They stared at their opponents. Bigger. Older. Meaner. The goal itself seemed such a long way away. They waited to be hurled into the frenzy of action that would decide their fate. Then the whistle blew. The ball was kicked. There was no more time to question or prepare. The game had begun. Val ran across the street and stepped into the open segment of the revolving door.

The door moved without any help from her. Trying to walk at its pace made her stumble as she entered the lobby. If she had been at school or at home, someone would have laughed. Here, no one did. Two men wearing black uniforms flicked their eyes at her. That quick glance was all they needed to see that she didn't belong.

Well, she didn't.

The lobby itself was three stories tall. A grand fireball was suspended from the ceiling.

"Star Tamer," she whispered. She couldn't wait to tell Tasman that she had guessed right.

Two walls of elevators were at the rear of the lobby, behind a barricade guarded by more men in green uniforms. Val watched a woman show a card to one of them. The man did something hidden behind a gleaming black counter. Magically the arms of the barricade parted and the woman passed through. Val considered the cards she had. Her school ID, her subway card, her library card, and the jack of diamonds. She doubted that any of them would work, even though Drew promised her the jack's magic powers would help her find money on the sidewalk. Still, she was digging through her backpack, looking for her cards, when one of the uniformed men stood over her. "Can I help you?"

Val thought of the clerk at that QXR clothing store. Val knew this man didn't want to help her, either—unless he could help her go away.

She stood up as tall as she could. "I would like to see Mr. Nuland of Geld Inc. Please," she added firmly.

She tried to be the model of a well-brought-up young lady. But the lobby's lights exposed the truth. Her shoes still had traces of mud from the last soccer match. Her shirt had grass stains her mom couldn't get out. And her right elbow had a big scab from when she dove to save the ball. That had been futile, too.

"Do you have an appointment?" the man said.

"No," Val admitted. But she didn't give up. "Can I make one?"

"I'm not Mr. Nuland's secretary."

"Can I see Mr. Nuland's secretary?"

"Do you have an appointment?"

Val didn't even ask if she could make one. She knew what the answer would be.

The man had been inching Val back toward the revolving door. When she felt the air whoosh behind her, she knew she was on the verge of being pushed out. She tried to dig her feet into the polished marble floor. If only she were wearing her cleats. If only she weren't the shortest and the youngest person in the building.

"I'll be back!" she shouted to the captured star.

The revolving door sucked her into one of its compartments. It carried her for a short distance and then cast her back out into the street.

Tasman wasn't waiting for Val outside the museum. Val sat down on the steps next to the base of the big statue of Teddy

Roosevelt riding a horse. She felt tired and discouraged. All she could do was pick at the dried mud on her shoe and hope he would get there soon.

Finally he came running up. He had on snow boots instead of the old slippers. He skidded across the pavement and tried to catch his breath. He looked so upset, she asked, "What happened?"

"Nothing," he said as he fell onto the step next to her. "Actually I shouldn't say that. Something did happen. Something always happens. Even if the world didn't spin anymore, that 'nothing' would actually cause a series of catastrophic somethings. Collisions. Oceans sloshing. Earthquakes. The toppling of the Captain's books. But more importantly, did you succeed in your quest?"

Val shook her head. "I couldn't even get in to see him."

"Ah. The Star Tamer dwells in an impenetrable fortress. We should have anticipated that. It's only the weak who are defenseless."

"The guard asked if I had an appointment."

"That's what they always say. The clock and the calendar are how they keep their distance. Never fear. Even a Star Tamer must leave his fortress eventually. And when he does, we will pounce." Tasman jumped, but he didn't make a very good cat. He landed awkwardly on the steps. Val grabbed his arm to keep him from falling.

She could feel how tense he was, even through the

fabric of his shirt. Touching him made her tense, too. So she let go.

"Thank you for saving me," he said.

Val sighed. If only it were that easy to save Lanora. She glanced across the street at the tall buildings on the far side of Central Park. The rays of the setting sun made some of the windows glow, as if they belonged to the realm of the Star Tamer. "We'll never get the things we need to make her whole," Val whispered.

"I'm surprised at you. Such sentiments from our heroine. Do I need to hurl clichés at you?"

"No," she said.

"It's always darkest before the dawn. If there's a will, there's a way."

"Stop." She threatened him with her fist.

He ran down the steps, calling back to her. "When the going gets tough, the tough get going."

She chased him all the way around the side of the museum. She finally tackled him on the grass, not far from the dog run. "Where did you get those chirpy slogans?"

"Haven't you ever been in a social worker's office?"

"Have you?" Val leaned on her elbow to study his face.

Tasman stood up and looked down at her. "I had an amazing insight. You are a girl." He offered his hand to pull her up.

She slapped it out of the way and jumped to her feet.

"No, no. You are. You may not suffer from the more ab-surd characteristics. You don't suck the ends of your hair, or check your appearance in the mirror, or squeal when con-fronted with small insects. But you are a girl."

"Your point?"

"Daughters don't need appointments."

"You want to ask Lanora to help with her own spell?"

"No. You can pretend to be Lanora."

This idea was terrible. Val didn't want to be Lanora, even if she could have managed it. "Mr. Nuland will know. Lanora has long auburn hair. I have short blonde hair."

"I know. But by then, you're in, you see?"

Val picked up a rock and tossed it from hand to hand. "Maybe."

"I'll help you practice. Come on. I'll be the secretary."

Tasman stood behind a park bench and pretended as if he were typing. He paused to apply lipstick.

"What are you doing?"

"Getting in character. You should, too. To begin with, would Lanora be playing with a rock?"

Val pretended to throw it at him. Then she dropped it to the ground. How should she be Lanora? She passed her hand over her face and tried to make a mask where her smile had been. Then she glided over to where Tasman was now chatting into an imaginary phone.

"And then you von't belief vat he do next," Tasman said.

"Why are you talking in a Russian accent?"

"It's Romanian. And stay in character. Approach again." Tasman pushed Val away. So Val pushed him back. Except he sidestepped her so she stumbled and fell. He sat on her legs and caught her flailing fists.

"This is *not* how Lanora would behave."

"How do you know? You never met her." With great effort, Val wriggled out from under Tasman. She was just about to knock him down again when she froze.

"What is it?" Tasman turned to see what Val was staring at.

"It's Lanora."

Lanora had heard them from Columbus Avenue, an entire block away. Everybody in the whole world could have. Laughing and goofing around like little kids. She had tried to ignore them. She had tried very hard to act like she was ignoring them. Then Val had walked around in a lame way. With her face all grim and her legs like they were half-paralyzed. It was so embarrassing. And then they said her name. Because that pathetic person Val was imitating was supposed to be Lanora.

Why didn't anyone stop them? Where were the grown-ups? The meddling moms? The security guards? Why had Lanora been caught and humiliated for taking a toy cat when these two kids were killing her?

But no one came, so Lanora had to make them stop. She stomped down the driveway where the buses brought the schoolchildren. She put her hands on her hips and tried to shoot death rays from her eyes.

Finally they noticed her. At first Val looked uncertain. Then she whispered to Tasman. Tasman stared at Lanora, as if she were some sort of specimen he was studying.

Lanora tried to smile like she didn't care what they thought. Why should she? They had dirt on their shirts from rolling around on the ground!

Now they were coming toward her. Why were they doing that? They were smiling again. How could they still be laughing at her? She refused to be mocked or pitied or scorned just because of a toy cat.

"Hi," Val said.

What kind of a thing was that to say? It would have been better if she said nothing, like the other day. But no. Val said "hi" as if nothing had happened. Like she was pretending Lanora's world hadn't come to an end. Val had become cruel, now that she had a boyfriend. Obviously Val didn't know that Tasman was a failed explorer.

Lanora tried to toss her hair back over her shoulder. The

wind interfered, whipping her hair across her face. She spat the strands out of her mouth. She turned on her heel. She was glad she had been practicing that in her bedroom. She spun a perfect 180. Despite the uneven ground, despite the wobbling inside, she didn't fall. She succeeded in walking away.

Twenty-eight

On Thursday after school, Val met Tasman in the shadow of the Geld Building.

"So that's the Star Tamer's Tower." Tasman stared up at the skyscraper as if he were trying to find a way to comprehend its overwhelming mass. "You know, I may have translated the passage in *The Book of Dares* incorrectly. It's possible that you're supposed to get a gift from a Tar Tamer. In which case, we should be looking for a man who is fixing roads."

"Maybe it was Scar Tamer?" Val said.

"A plastic surgeon! And speaking of appearances, you look nice. Very Lanora-esque."

"I did my best." Val looked down at herself. She didn't own any skirts, but she had put on actual pants. Her shirt had colorful stripes and no sports team logo or number across her back.

"Do you want me to go in the lobby with you?" Tasman said.

Val didn't answer right away.

"This is where you're supposed to say, 'No, of course not. I will go bravely into battle while you stay out here keeping a lookout.' Even though there's nothing actually dangerous on the street. Except perhaps whatever is being sold by that hot dog vendor."

"Just wish me luck."

He waggled his fingers mysteriously and then bonked her head with his fist.

Val quickly crossed the street. It was kind of hard to walk fast. Her ballet flats had slippery soles. She adjusted her pace so she could approach the revolving door at precisely the moment a chamber appeared. Yes, she said to herself as she walked through easily. As if she had done so every day.

That was the trick. She had to act as if she belonged in this cold, glittering realm. She couldn't look up at the exploding light fixture suspended three stories above her head. She had to treat the Tamed Star like it was just an old bunch of bulbs.

She didn't wait to be approached by the guards. She glided over to the desk and announced, "I'm here to see my father, Mr. Nuland."

"Is he expecting you?" the keeper of the book said.

"I'm Lanora Nuland," Val said, with what she hoped was disdain.

"I'm sorry, but I don't see any instructions from Mr. Nuland's secretary."

"He will *not* be happy if you turn me away," Val said.

The specter of an angry Star Tamer made a dark cloud. The keeper of the book filled out a name tag with her name and destination. He handed it to Val and performed a secret ceremony under the counter. The metal arms slid back into their mounts. The way was clear. Val was tempted to run to her goal, but she made herself walk all the way to the elevator. Her heels tapped confidently against the glistening floor.

The elevator doors parted. She entered and pressed the button. She rose up and up and up. At least she assumed she did; the ride was so smooth she could have been standing still. The doors opened. She left the elevator and walked briskly to a large table at the end of a corridor.

A beautiful woman sat in front of a computer screen and an arrangement of twisted stems in a crystal vase.

"Lanora," the woman purred. "How nice to see you. I'm sorry, but your father is in a meeting now. I can take a message, if you like."

Think fast, Val. The ball is coming. Choose the teammate who is open and has the best chance for a goal. Quick! Quick!

"I will wait in his office." Val walked briskly away from the woman.

"I'm sorry, but you can't—"

Val saw no need to argue with the woman. Val was going, so obviously she could. The corridor divided; Val had to guess right or left. The odds were fifty-fifty. She headed away from the brighter lights and toward the bigger doors.

A man walked by without looking at her. He was busy with his phone.

Was that Mr. Nuland? The man wore a nice suit. He had short hair. He was tall. These men all looked alike. These men were all Star Tamers, or Assistant Star Tamers. What if Val couldn't recognize the particular one she needed?

She passed shut doors. She passed offices with big desks and leather chairs. She kept walking. She was a hunter in the forest. She was on high alert. She would recognize her prey. She had no idea how, but she would. Didn't he have Lanora's steel gray eyes?

More people passed her. They didn't pay any attention to her. Maybe she was wearing a cloak of invisibility. Then a man's voice called, "Lanora?"

She didn't look back. He sounded like one of the guards.

"Lanora, can I speak with you for just a moment?"

Val had reached the end of the corridor. There was no exit. She pushed open a door and stepped inside.

The room was unoccupied. On the desk were a phone and a computer. Opposite the desk were two leather chairs. An abstract painting dominated the wall above a sleek cabinet. That was all. Did anyone ever sit at that desk? Val thought of her mom's office, with its pictures of her family, the goofy cartoons stuck to the side of the computer, the pencils in a jar decorated by Drew, the dish of candy, and the books everywhere. Mom didn't have a window. But this office had four, two on each side of the corner. The view was unbelievable. New York sprawled at her feet. How unreal the world seemed, without people or sounds or smells.

She turned away from the window to get her focus back. The ball was in her possession, but not for long. The other team was bearing down on her.

Maybe she could take something from this office. Maybe something belonging to any old Star Tamer could be the gift. She looked for a small item. Even the trash basket was empty. She would have to take a chair. Or maybe the picture from the wall.

The door opened.

A minion came in. "Lanora, your father has just made reservations for you and a friend at tonight's performance of *Sleeping Beauty*. You'd better run along."

Val gritted her teeth. What made her so mad? The words "run along"? The bribe? The choice of show? The knowledge that if the real Lanora were given those tickets, she wouldn't have picked Val as the friend to take? Or maybe it was everything—the office and the tower and the guards and the assumption that she would do what they wanted. Well, they were wrong.

Val sat on the desk chair and locked her arms around its arms, just like when she and her mom had joined with other protestors to make a human chain in front of City Hall. "I need to see my father, Mr. Nuland."

Saying that name seemed to conjure a voice from the hall. "Can't you people handle this?"

Mr. Nuland strode into the room. He stopped and stared at Val for a moment. He wasn't sure why he didn't recognize his daughter.

"I'm Val."

"Val?" This puzzled him even more. He might have understood why his own daughter would disrupt his work, but not his daughter's friend. "Why are *you* here?"

"Because we have to save Lanora."

The words "save Lanora" were blazed across the sky. They were scratched into the plate-glass window. They hung in the room like a cloud of smoke. At least, that was how it seemed to Val. Nothing could be plainer than this. Nothing more important.

But Mr. Nuland was a grown-up. Like all grown-ups, he had a very short attention span. He checked the heavy gold manacle on his wrist that chained him to time and money. He was shocked by how much of each he had wasted on this situation. He shook his head and made a little clicking sound in his throat.

"Don't you understand?" Val said.

As a matter of fact, he didn't. Many grown-ups say one thing and mean another, so they assume that kids aren't speaking the truth, either. Mr. Nuland believed that when Val said "We need to save Lanora," she really meant "I won't go away until you give me a treat."

"Miss Campbell, what do we have that our young friend might like? Coffee? Tea?"

Val stared at him.

He couldn't meet her eyes. He adjusted his tie. He checked his watch again. "Miss Campbell, I know you girls keep a supply of candy in your desks."

He patted Miss Campbell in such a way to push her from the office. He tried to do the same to Val. "Go along with Miss Campbell. Thanks so much for stopping by. But now I really must get back to work."

"That won't help Lanora." Val folded her arms and kept her ground.

The other adults in the room trembled. They were right to be afraid. Even though Mr. Nuland couldn't touch Val, he could attack them. And he did, dispatching them from the room with one sharp glance.

Miss Campbell returned with a golden box of special chocolates that she had been carefully rationing to last the rest of the month. She held the open box under Val's nose. The pieces of chocolate were set like jewels in gold paper. Each one was handmade, embossed with a crest, as if to proclaim that they were the property of kings.

Val had never seen candy like this before. She doubted that she ever would again. The candy she usually got was wrapped in plastic paper and sold at any corner store. She licked her lips as she wondered how this deluxe kind would taste.

Mr. Nuland took the box from Miss Campbell and moved it enticingly to lure Val closer to the door.

Val followed. Then she grabbed the back of the chair and slowly shook her head at Mr. Nuland.

"What kid doesn't like chocolate?" He took a piece and popped it into his mouth. He swallowed it whole, without even tasting it. Miss Campbell sighed at the waste.

"The gift has to come from you." Val pointed to him.

"From me? I don't have any candy. I've got cigars. Ha ha ha. Would you like a cigar?"

"Is that what you think will save Lanora?" Val didn't like how her voice cracked with emotion. She needed to stay grounded. She had to hold the line and fight to get the ball back.

The Book of Dares had said the Star Tamer's gift must prove his devotion. Maybe Val needed to be clearer. "She needs to know you care."

"Care! Of course I care!" He spluttered. "Greywacke Academy costs fifty thousand a year. That's just for tuition. She'll still need room and board. She could go to Harvard for less than this will cost me."

Val's mouth went dry. So it was done. Lanora was enrolled at reform school. "How can you just send her away?"

"Don't blame me. I didn't steal that stuffed cat." He flung his arms wildly in the air. "Can you believe it? All this trouble is because of a cat? I could have bought her a hundred of them, if that was what she wanted. Only she didn't really. She just wanted to humiliate me. To make me suffer." He thumped himself on the chest.

"It isn't about you," Val said, a little more loudly than she'd intended.

Mr. Nuland pulled his sleeve down and adjusted his watch. "Of course not. It's about what's best for Lanora. That's why she's going there on Sunday. She needs experts who can help her."

Val looked at her shoes. The little ballet flats pinched her toes. She wanted to kick something. Sadly there wasn't anything she could kick. Mr. Nuland was right. Lanora needed experts. Not some crazy words from *The Book of Dares*.

The game was over. Val had lost. She walked over to Mr. Nuland. She always shook her opponent's hand. Even if they had fought dirty and talked trash and in general not been good sports at all. She held out her hand to Mr. Nuland. As he took it, she looked into his eyes. They were exactly like Lanora's eyes.

The outside was cool gray, and in control. Something flickered across the center, like a little bird beating against the glass, trying to get out to where it could fly. She remembered how hurt Lanora had been yesterday in the park. Val felt awful about that. She knew it was wrong to abandon her friend. So she hung on no matter how hard Mr. Nuland tried to pull away. Her fingers squeezed his fingers. Her feet slipped inside her shoes. Her heart pounded as she struggled. As she held Mr. Nuland's hand, she felt the pulse of his heart, too.

"She needs to *know* you care," Val said again.

"But how?" he said softly.

"Do you tell her?"

Mr. Nuland looked out the window, at the glorious view. "It's hard to talk to her."

"I know. It's hard for me, too." Val was ashamed of the idiotic way she had said "hi" yesterday. "You still have to try. We all have to try."

He nodded. "I will. I'm very glad you came."

"Me, too." Val released him from her grip and headed

for the door. Then she stopped. She had almost forgotten she still needed something from the Star Tamer. "I've changed my mind. I think I would like a cigar."

He took one from his pocket. He bowed as he ceremoniously handed it to her.

She bowed, too. Then she took off those slippery shoes so she could run out of the office.

Twenty-nine

Val waved the cigar triumphantly as she ran out of the glass tower and across the street. "I got it! I got it!"

Tasman was standing with the hot dog man. "She returns victorious. Didn't I tell you she would? She is intrepid."

Val wasn't sure what that meant, but it sounded like praise, so she smiled.

"Val, I'd like you to meet Akmed. He is from Egypt. He has climbed the Great Pyramid. He has sailed a felucca on the Nile. He has walked among the ruins at Luxor. He has seen places that I must only imagine. They remain forever beyond my reach, on the opposite end of the Earth."

Akmed bowed humbly. "There is, here in your city, a gift from my country. It stands taller than the trees of the park, behind the Metropolitan Museum of Art."

"You mean Cleopatra's Needle?" Val said. "You can see the top of it from the baseball fields."

"A needle? No. It's a large piece of granite, seventy feet tall, weighing two hundred twenty-four tons. It has nothing to do with Cleopatra. It's from the time of Thutmose III. 1450 B.C." Akmed said.

"That's a thousand years older than Cleopatra," Tasman said.

"She is the most famous queen of Egypt, but Egypt had many great rulers," Akmed said.

"Ramesses II was the most powerful pharaoh of all. He built many temples and cities throughout Egypt," Tasman said.

"Ramesses II had inscriptions carved into the obelisk. 'Ramesses II. Chosen of Ra. Like the Sun, Life-Giving Forever,'" Akmed said.

"I didn't know it was so amazing," Val said.

Akmed smiled. "Your city contains much that no one ever sees."

"That is true," Tasman said sadly. Then he turned to Val. "But we could go there, couldn't we?"

"You want to go to the park?" Val said.

"I don't want to. But I will. When everything is ready. When the time is right," Tasman said.

They said good-bye to Akmed and headed north on Park Avenue.

"Why don't you like the park?" Val said.

Tasman chose that moment to duck around a woman talking on her cell phone.

When Val caught up to him, she said, "I would think you'd love it. The paths curve all around in crazy ways, just like the way your mind works."

"That's the trouble. The paths aren't in straight lines. Just when you think you are safe, you discover that you've been brought very near to a dangerous place, where you never intended to go."

They had reached the entrance to the subway. Tasman stopped at the top of the stairs leading down to the tunnels.

"We need the last thing," Val said. "I found out that Lanora is supposed to start reform school on Monday."

"We only have three days left," Tasman said. " 'Finally I bring from my own heart, the origin of the ministering wind.' "

"Whatever that means," Val said.

"You're supposed to know your own heart," Tasman said.

"I know I can't wait to take all the things to Lanora's apartment."

"You mean, stick them in one of those brightly colored gifty bags and hang it on her doorknob?"

Val shrugged. She had kind of thought that. Except she

was going to put them in a reusable shopping bag. Her mom had dozens.

Tasman shook his head. "Your brother is right. You don't know much about these things."

Val showed him the cigar again. She knew enough to get it.

"There has to be a ceremony," Tasman said.

"What kind of ceremony?" Val said.

"Saturday night. At midnight we shall stand astride the crack between the days and wrestle with whatever demons crawl out into the world. We will go to the obelisk and pay our respects to the sun god Ra, the giver of life."

Val was shocked. "You'd go in the park at midnight?"

"If I can, yes. Yes, I would do that. Assuming that certain other conditions have been met."

Val looked down the stairs. They were well lit. Lots of people rushed down without giving them a second thought. She herself had ridden the subways her whole life. She knew that there was nothing to be afraid of down there. Still, her heart pounded as she looked toward the darkness.

"You know, we could do the ceremony someplace else. Maybe by the store where she stole the cat. Or maybe by school. Or maybe the laundry room of my building. Hardly anybody goes there."

"No. This isn't a game, you know. We have to take it seriously or it won't work."

Val nodded. "Okay. The obelisk on Saturday night."

Tasman clasped her hand.

Then together they walked down toward darkness.

Thirty

The night was full of possibilities. Most humans didn't know that. They preferred to stay indoors near artificial lights. To them, the dark just meant it was time for sleep. And so they never saw what cats saw, heard what cats heard, or sensed what cats sensed.

Mau listened for a moment. The sounds of traffic were closer than she thought. Cars honked their horns. Dogs barked. The subway trains rumbled underneath. None of these noises were unusual. But something was not as it should be. And so Mau crossed the street and ran down another alley.

The brochure lay on the kitchen table. Lanora didn't touch it. She didn't need to open it up to read what was inside. The picture told her everything she needed to know about where she was headed on Sunday. The gray stone building looked as impenetrable as a medieval fortress. The field of green grass had been clipped painfully short. The smiling young man and the smiling young woman were clad in ill-fitting burgundy blazers. A guarantee was made in bold lettering:

GREYWACKE ACADEMY
Where Everyone Succeeds

Presumably even someone like Lanora.

Now Lanora had no quarrel with success. She wanted nothing less. She was certain her definition wasn't the same as Greywacke Academy's.

She walked slowly into her bedroom and shut the door.

"Sweetheart? I know you don't need to pack quite yet, but I think you should at least look over the list."

Lanora could imagine what was on it.

Multiple pairs of underwear and white ankle socks.

White blouses.

Flannel nightgowns.

Every article of clothing carefully labeled LANORA NU-LAND so that she could never accidentally lose the things she despised.

There would be another list—of forbidden objects.

Nail polish. Blow-dryers. Jewelry. Anything that could distinguish her from the others.

Scissors. Fingernail files. Belts. Shoelaces. Anything that might pose a suicide risk.

"Sweetheart? Your father won't like it if we leave things until the last minute."

Lanora opened her window and climbed out onto her fire escape.

She wished she could see Mau. She hadn't seen Mau in days. What if she had to go without saying good-bye? She knew she would miss Mau more than anything. It was highly unlikely that there would be any cats at Greywacke Academy. Plenty of rats, however. Plenty of vermin to gnaw at Lanora's brain.

She gripped the railing and leaned over the platform as far as she dared. Sometimes Mau came in the alley at night. For a moment Lanora thought Mau was at the bottom of the tree, getting ready to climb up to see her. But the black shape was a plastic bag. The wind played with it for a while. It flew up in the sky, as if it were a bird. Then the wind abandoned the bag and let it fall to the ground as trash.

Yes, trash.

She hadn't meant for any of this to happen. Somehow, one thing followed another, and now she was headed to Greywacke Academy.

But she wasn't there yet. She climbed up the ladder-like stairs of the fire escape. For some reason, she thought of Val. Val loved it out here. She hung down from the steps by her knees. Val laughed when Lanora called her a monkey. And Lanora had laughed, too.

It seemed like such a long time ago. Much longer than last summer.

How had Val done it?

Lanora held on to the railing on the left side with both hands. Then she eased herself around the edge until she was alongside the ladder. She reached below the ladder and made a quick grab for the railing on the right side. Now she had one hand on each railing, but her feet were resting on the steps. She took a deep breath and let her legs hang down in empty space.

Now she was free.

Yes, free, of her mom's sighs.

Free of Tasman's eyes.

Free of everything she had done and everything she didn't do.

Free of wanting her father's praise.

Free of being afraid of his displeasure.

Free of her fear of falling.

She could let go of the railing. Why not? She had let so much else go.

The wind stirred.

Mrrrow! A cat cried in alarm. A black blur raced up the tree and leapt onto the platform beside Lanora's dangling legs.

Mrrow!

"Is that you, Mau?"

Lanora began trembling as soon as she saw the cat coming toward her. The muscles in her arms quivered as she looped her legs back around the rusty railing. She rested there for a moment before she had the strength to crawl back down to where Mau sat on the platform.

Mau climbed into Lanora's arms. It wasn't entirely clear who held whom. Mau gripped Lanora's shoulder with her claws. She let Lanora stroke her, even though that was contrary to every principle for preserving the dignity of a cat. But Mau stayed where she was. After all, this was an extraordinary circumstance. Besides, the gentle pressure was pleasant.

Then Mau felt something surprising land on her fur. Drops of moisture?

Mau looked up at the sky. There were no clouds. She could see the moon. So how then could it be raining?

Ah. Then Mau understood. This must be that peculiar human trait known as tears.

Thirty-one

The park was off-limits at dusk, much less at midnight. How would Val persuade her parents that she needed to go there on Saturday night? Could she tell them the truth—that she needed to stand astride the crack of midnight and wrestle with the demons that crawled out into the world? Or should she say, "Hey, Mom and Dad, I need to spend the night with this kid I know"? Except that she didn't know Tasman since he never answered questions with a simple fact. Instead he babbled obscure words like he had memorized the dictionary. To make the situation worse, he was a boy. Her parents might be suspicious that Val wanted to spend the night with him for another reason. When she didn't think of him like that. At least, she didn't think she did.

There was no way around it. Val needed to lie. This bothered her. It bothered her even more that she couldn't use the lie that would have been so easy even two months ago. "Spending the night at Lanora's," she could have said. That would have been that. No need to check with Mrs. Nuland whether it was okay. It was always okay. The only thing her mom would do was send along fruit and bagels. Breakfast was a haphazard event at Lanora's house.

But Val couldn't say that. If she did, her mom would have jumped on the topic. How *is* Lanora? What counseling is she getting? Has she started her community service yet? Would she like the name of a support group? How is Mrs. Nuland? Would *she* like the name of a support group? The questions would be endless. No, Val had to ask someone else to be part of this lie.

The soccer team wouldn't approve. They didn't want her doing anything extracurricular. But she did know some girls who might understand.

At lunchtime on Friday, she went to find the Poetry Club.

"Why, look. It's Val," Helena said.

"Is it raining?" Olivia said.

"No. She has something to say. Her face is an open book," Gillian said.

"Which page? Table of contents?" Tina said.

"Acknowledgments?" Gillian said.

"Copyright info?" Helena said.

"Don't torment her. Let her speak," Olivia said.

Val took out her sandwich. Today there were no googly

eyes to make her laugh. No cootie catcher to predict the future. Just a note from her mom. *Love you! Thanks for being you!* Val folded it up quickly and put it away.

"If a picture is worth one thousand words. Dot dot dot," Helena said.

"Isn't it ten thousand?" Tina said.

"Inflation?" Gillian said.

"Deflation. Since now words can be initials. LOL," Helena said.

"TTYL," Olivia said.

"WWVS," Gillian said.

"Q?" Tina said.

"What Would Val Say?" Gillian said.

They stared at Val, waiting, chins resting on their fists.

"I need to spend the night on Saturday," Val said.

"We can be at my house," Helena said.

"Your mom won't mind?" Val said.

"She's dead," Helena said.

"I'm so sorry." Val was shocked. This didn't seem like a very good omen.

"It's okay. My sister does the role-play. On one condition." Helena leaned forward and whispered. "You have to tell me why."

Val didn't know how to answer that.

"Let me guess. You are evicted," Tina said.

"Homeless," Gillian said.

"Orphaned," Olivia said.

"No. I don't need to, I just need to *seem* to," Val said.

"Ah. Romance." They all nodded.

"It's nothing like that." Val nervously picked the seeds off the crust of her whole-grain sandwich. Then she carefully put each one back in the plastic bag. Lying always made enough of a mess. "I need to go to the obelisk in Central Park at midnight on Saturday and perform a ritual from *The Book of Dares*."

"Whoa," Tina said.

"That is the best," Gillian said.

"I'm writing it down," Helena said.

"You can't use Val's image," Olivia said.

"Why not? She'll never make a poem out of it," Helena said.

"Who is the guy?" Olivia said.

"How did you meet?" Helena said.

"No one worth lying for goes to this school," Gillian said.

"Maybe it's a girl," Tina said.

"A girl? Way to go, Val," Olivia said.

"No," Val said. "I really am going to the obelisk to perform a ritual."

The poets raised their eyebrows.

"Do you mean metaphorically?" Helena said.

Val shook her head.

"And the reason is?" Helena said.

"Please don't say it's for your science project," Tina said.

Val shook her head.

"Then it really is a spell?" Olivia said.

The poets all clasped hands. "We are there."

"But it's private," Val said.

"Who cares?" Tina said.

"You've already told us where you're going to be," Helena said.

Obviously lying was more complicated than Val thought. Before she spoke to her parents, she decided to prepare. She wrote some talking points on a piece of paper. She glanced at it under the table after her family all sat down to dinner.

Drew banged his spoon against all the dishes he could reach. "I have an announcement."

"What?" Dad grabbed the hand with the spoon. Mom carefully took his fork, too.

"I decided what to be for Halloween."

This was serious business. If you wore a costume every day of the year, what could you do for Halloween? Last year Drew had driven the whole family crazy with impossible plans. He wanted to be a dragon with actual fire-breathing capabilities. He wanted to be the Staten Island Ferry with cars that could drive off and on his ramp. He wanted to be the universe. No wonder Mom and Dad were worried.

"I considered the Mars Rover," Drew said.

"Excellent choice. I think even I can make that," Mom said.

"But I can't be the Mars Rover because some people have forgotten to do something extremely important." Drew stared at Val.

"What people?" Dad said.

Drew straightened his cape. "Because those people have not kept their promises, I have to be The One Who Saves Lanora."

"No, you don't," Val said.

"I do. I'm going to have a special hat with feathers. And I'm going to have a shield and a harness with a big, sharp sword."

"Why do you need a sharp sword?" Mom didn't like weapons.

"Because I have to punish Werd for doing this to Lanora."

"Maybe you could let his guardians punish him?" Mom said.

"No. Justice must be done. It isn't fair that Lanora is suffering and nothing bad is happening to Werd."

Val squeezed the paper with her talking points in her fist. Drew was right. It wasn't fair that the A Team just la-la-la-ed along. The worst that had happened to them was that her mom had scolded them for eating grapes.

"Do you know what karma is?" Dad said.

"Yes. Karma is when you're in a car with your ma. And something makes her mad. Like another car going too fast. And your dad says, 'Don't worry. They won't get away with that.' And sure enough, you go around another hill and there they are in the ditch," Drew said.

"Sort of," Dad said.

"Except I don't get mad," Mom said.

"Oh, no," Dad said.

Mom made a face at him. "The point is that you don't have to punish anybody. Karma takes care of that."

"What about saving? Who takes care of that?" Drew said.

Val moved some food around on her plate.

"Because I've been waiting a very, very, very long time for some saving to happen," Drew said.

Val didn't like being scolded by her brother. She had been trying her best to get it done. "You won't have to wait much longer."

"I won't? What are you going to do?" Drew said excitedly.

She obviously couldn't tell him about the ceremony, so she decided to make her other announcement. She glanced at the piece of paper. "On Saturday we're all sleeping over at Helena's so we can work on poetry about issues facing kids today. Kids like Lanora."

"Poetry?" Mom said.

"Poetry?" Dad said.

"Poetry?" Drew said.

"What's wrong with poetry?" Val said.

"Nothing. It's just so unlike you," Dad said.

"How do you know what I'm like? I'm in middle school now," Val said.

"My super mind-reader can probe your secrets." Drew grabbed the closest fork and spoon and stuck them out from his eyes. He swiveled his head and scanned the room. *"Beep, beep, beep."* He faced his mom and said in a mechanical voice, "Do not get sauce on your yellow shirt."

Mom laughed and tried to give him a fork that wasn't dripping.

Drew swiveled around and pointed at Dad. *"Beep, beep, beep. I wish I had one of those devices."*

Dad laughed. "He's right. I do."

Then he pointed at Val and said, *"Beep, beep, beep. Lanora, Lanora, Lanora. Tasman."*

"Who is Tasman?" Mom said.

"Nobody." Val took her plate into the kitchen and turned on the faucet to wash it.

She heard her parents quizzing Drew. Who was Tasman?

The water spiraled down the drain. Who *was* Tasman? Why had she believed him?

She had followed the instructions. She had gathered the things with fire and spirit. (Well, everything except the gift from her own heart.) But what would she do when she was at the obelisk? What really would happen when the spirit had been restored, when *Archandara, Photaza, Zabythix*?

Would the doors be thrown open? Would Lanora take her place among those who are whole? Or would something else come out from the depths? Something that Tasman feared?

Thirty-two

On Saturday morning, Lanora's mom tapped on the door. "Wake up, sweetie," Emma said.

Lanora had been awake for hours, trying to figure out what she should do on her last whole day in New York City.

"Time to get up, Lanora," Emma said.

On Monday morning, Lanora wouldn't hear her mom's voice singing the syllables of her name. Something else would rouse her out of bed. A clanging bell? A buzzing alarm? The blast of a bugle?

"You can't lie in bed all morning. Today is the first day of the rest of your life."

That wasn't quite true. Today was the last day of her old life. Monday would be when her new life began. When she would put on her uniform and take her place among the other kids who had been sent away.

But today, she didn't have to wear the white button-down blouse or the pleated skirt. Today she could wear whatever she wanted.

She stood in front of her closet. She pulled out the gypsy skirt and the pirate shirt. She held them against her body, but she didn't put them on. Why dress up when she had no place to go? She put them in the large black trash bag that contained more clothes than her suitcase. She was being practical. There wasn't any point in keeping the things she could never wear again.

"Lanora?"

Her mom must have heard her moving about. Lanora put on a T-shirt and a pair of sweatpants and came out of her room.

"There you are. I'm glad you slept late today. Tomorrow we'll have to get an early start."

Lanora nodded. She went into the kitchen and got a bowl and a spoon.

"I have to go back to the store. The list says seven white blouses and I only bought five. You'd think you could wear something different on the weekend."

Emma smiled. Lanora smiled.

"I'll be back soon. Can you find some breakfast?" Emma said.

"Sure, Mom."

After her mom left, Lanora filled a bowl with a brown cereal that was supposed to help her lose weight and fight cholesterol, while supplying all the vitamins a girl needed. She dutifully ate what was good for her.

So what if other girls ate croissants with blackberry preserves as they anticipated a day of seizing whatever pleasures they wanted—provided the security guards weren't looking. Lanora didn't think about those girls whose names began with the letter A. She no longer wondered why they never got caught.

The cupboard door was open. She got up to shut it. Way at the back, in a forgotten zone, was a brightly colored box with a cheerful bird that didn't seem to mind at all that he was burdened by an enormous beak. Toucan Sam.

She reached into the box and took out a few pieces of cereal. She arranged the brightly colored circles into the order for a rainbow. Red orange yellow green blue violet. She ate an orange one. It tasted stale. That wasn't surprising. It had to be many years old. She decided she should preserve this artifact from a different era, from the period B.D.—before divorce. She carefully closed the box and carried it into her room. She put it in her suitcase. She would have to hide it somehow. But what if there were no private places? Not even under her bed?

The phone rang.

Her mom often called with a question. Could Lanora

take something out of the freezer? Could Lanora see if they needed another roll of toilet paper? Could Lanora measure how much milk was left in the gallon? Could Lanora reassure her mom that she hadn't gotten into any more trouble?

"What, Mom?" Lanora said.

Only it was her father who said, "Lanora?"

"Mom isn't home," Lanora said.

"I know. She called me from the store."

Lanora switched ears as she thought about what that meant. "So why are you calling?"

"Do I need a reason?"

Well, okay, he didn't *need* one. But he usually treated her like she was his assistant who had to do certain things for him. Get good grades and exercise and send thank-you notes.

"You always have some kind of agenda," she said.

"I guess that's why Val said . . ."

She switched ears again, this time glaring at the phone for a moment, as if it were Val. No, because it wasn't Val. Because Val didn't care that she was going away. Val was too busy with Tasman. "What does Val have to do with it?"

"Nothing. So. How are you?" he said.

How was she? Was there ever a more meaningless question? "Fine." A firm answer. With a big fat period after it.

"That's good." He sounded a little wistful.

Then there was silence. So she wondered, was there something else he was trying to say? If so, why didn't he just say it? He never had trouble telling her what to do before.

"Mom got everything on the list."

"The list?" He sounded puzzled.

"The Greywacke list. I'll be all ready to go tomorrow."

Suddenly she was eager to get out of there. Away from the tiny kitchen table always set for two. Away from the gap on the shelf where the mug she had decorated for him used to be. Away from the photographs Emma insisted on keeping on the refrigerator. All those little Lanoras. With no teeth. With rolls of fat. With peanut butter in her hair. Worst of all, the ones neatly cut in half. Emma couldn't bear to throw away the whole picture just because it made her sick to look at a certain someone's face.

"You might want to rent Mom a car with GPS. I can help her get to Greywacke, of course, but she'll need it for the return trip. She gets confused when she's upset."

"I could take you. Unless . . ."

Since his voice trailed away, she finished his sentence for him. "Unless you have to work. Because you always work on weekends. And if you have to go play golf or to the theater or out to brunch, then it's still work, isn't it, Dad?"

He made a strange sound. Then he cleared his throat and said, "I meant, unless you don't want to go."

"Don't want to?" She staggered backwards and bumped into the chair. She sat down on it. She held the phone in front of her so she could shout at it. "Like I have a choice?"

"But, honey, you *do* have a choice. You only think you don't. But you do. You don't have to go to Greywacke. All you have to do is . . ."

She hung up.

She looked at her feet. Her toenails were painted silver. The color of the actual shoes that Dorothy wore in the book *The Wizard of Oz*. The ones that had given her the power to get her wish. The ones that she had been wearing for practically the whole story before someone finally thought to tell her what the shoes could do.

Lanora clicked her heels together.

Nothing happened.

Then her mom came in. "I should have bought the blouses before. They didn't have your size so I had to go to a different store. It was much more expensive. So I called your father because you know how he is about things like that."

"Yes. I know."

Lanora went into her room. She took the box of Fruit Loops out of her suitcase and put it in the trash bag with all the other things she wouldn't be needing at Greywacke or ever again.

Thirty-three

All during the soccer practice on Saturday, Val had to keep retying her shoes. She was much more nervous than before a big game. With good reason. There had been no practice for the ceremony tonight! No game simulation. No drills. No endless repetition of the corner kick. She had never gone to the obelisk in the middle of the night with just a few scraggly feathers, a smelly cigar, an old bowl (if Tasman found it), and some other object she hadn't even figured out yet.

She said good-bye to her teammates and walked home. The sun shone so brightly, it seemed impossible to believe that in just a few hours, they would be at the mercy of the moon. Now the sky was blue. The leaves were green. The colors of the kids' clothing seemed to dance before her eyes. This world was so crowded with sights and sounds and smells; there didn't seem to be space for demons and spells.

What if the ceremony didn't work?

What if it did?

After a dinner she could hardly eat, Val went into her room to pack. She tried to stick her sleeping bag inside her backpack.

Drew handed her a small, fuzzy purple rabbit.

"What's this for?" Val said.

"Just in case you miss me. I know I'm irreplaceable, but I held the bunny under my armpit for thirty seconds. That should be long enough for some of my powers to be stuck in its fuzz."

"You mean your smell?" She taunted him with it.

"Don't wave it around. It's losing strength. Stick it in your bag."

She hugged the rabbit. She wondered if she could bring something from her parents, too.

Her mom knocked and came into the room. "I just talked with Helena's mother."

Val turned away to put the rabbit in her backpack. Her mom couldn't have spoken with Helena's mom. She was dead. Val should have remembered that her mom would call Helena's mom. Now Val was trapped by her lie.

"She sounded quite strict," Mom said.

Val sighed with relief. Helena's sister must have pretended.

"I hope she's not so much of a worrier that you won't have any fun," Mom said.

Val smiled. No one worried more than her own mom. So Val hugged her.

"What's this? You're not nervous about going, are you?" Mom said.

"Are you nervous?" Drew said.

"I started spending the night with kids when I was eight," Val said.

"I know. But it's different than going to Lanora's, isn't it?" Mom smoothed Val's yellow hair behind her ears. "You won't know where the bathroom is."

"Mo-om," Val said.

"Well, you won't," Mom said.

"They might not even have a bathroom," Drew said.

"Everybody has a bathroom," Val said.

"Astronauts don't. They wear diapers!" Drew rolled on the floor laughing.

"I better finish packing," Val said.

"Aren't you done?" Mom said.

"Not quite." Val hadn't chosen the third thing. "Maybe you could find us some cookies?"

"Yes, maybe you could find *us* some cookies?" Drew said.

"Of course, sweetie. I didn't want to assume that Helena's

mom—or dad—didn't bake. I'll go get some right now." Mom patted Val's arm and steered Drew to the kitchen.

Val looked around her room in a panic. She hadn't wanted to leave the third thing until the last minute. She just couldn't decide. What was a gift from her own heart? What was the origin of the ministering wind? What was a ministering wind? Most winds seemed cold, and not the least bit caring.

"Are you ready? We're going to walk you," Dad called.

"Walk me?" Val stuck her head out of her room.

"It's already getting dark," Mom said.

So it was. Val had to hurry. She yanked open each of her desk drawers. What could it be? A picture of her and Lanora? The orange butterfly dangle? Neither of these things seemed important enough. Books, drawings, jewelry she never wore, socks, shirts, what could it be?

A golden soccer medal hung from its red ribbon on a hook. Val took it down and read the inscription: Most Valuable Player. She had won it last year for saving the most goals. She carefully wrapped the ribbon around the golden disk and put it in the small pocket of her backpack next to the cigar.

As she came out of her room, Drew shone a flashlight in her face and then his own. "See or be seen?"

"He's not coming, too, is he?" Val said.

"Of course he is," Drew said.

"Nighttime walk," Dad said.

Drew raced down the stairs. The rest of the family took the elevator because of the sleeping bag, the backpack, and a large canvas bag.

"I just said a few cookies," Val said.

"I know, but I had a lot of fruit. And a big bottle of green tea. It isn't cold, but you could pour it over ice," Mom said.

Dad nudged Val.

"Thanks, Mom," Val said.

Drew shone the big light in their faces as the elevator door opened. "Beat you!"

He ran outside the lobby. The beam of his flashlight attacked the side of the building. *Bam bam pshooo pshoo argghhhh.*

"It's too bad we have to have all these streetlights," Mom said.

"You want it to be dark?" Val's voice cracked a little.

"Wouldn't it be nice to walk outside at night and see stars?" Mom said.

Val looked up. The clouds moved above her at a dizzying pace.

"Would one night a year be too much to ask?" Mom said.

"On that night, it would probably be cloudy," Dad said.

"Drew, wait at the corner!" Mom called.

Drew turned back and held his flashlight under his chin.

Val gasped. The sculpted shadows revealed an entirely different face. Old and ghoulish, and maybe even evil.

Drew shone the flashlight on his family as he danced impatiently from foot to foot. "Hurry up. They're waiting."

Val wondered why he had said "they." He must have meant the girls at the party. He couldn't know about Tasman. Or the spirits that they were intent upon summoning out of the dark.

She moved around her dad to be near the hand that wasn't holding the sleeping bag, just in case she needed to grab on.

As they got closer to Helena's building, Val kept a lookout for Tasman. She was worried that Drew would see him and spoil everything. Then she worried when she didn't see Tasman. What if he had been unable to get the incantation bowl? What if he wasn't going to come? Would she dare to go into the park by herself?

"Is this it?" Dad said.

Mom marched toward where the light spilled out from the lobby.

Val stayed on the sidewalk. "You don't have to go up."

"It's only polite to say hello," Mom said.

"We won't embarrass you," Dad said.

"It isn't that," Val said.

"What's wrong, honey?" Mom said.

Val wanted to tell them everything. Everything! If she

did, they could all go home, and Dad would make jokes and Mom would make popcorn and Drew would make trouble.

"I can go the rest of the way by myself," Val said.

Her parents exchanged the look that meant, She's not our little girl anymore.

"Okay, then." Dad put down the sleeping bag and hugged Val.

Then Mom hugged Dad hugging Val. "I know you'll be polite and helpful."

Would being polite and helpful keep Val out of danger?

Drew didn't join the sandwich. He waited so that he could whisper in Val's ear. "Good luck." As if he knew what she hoped would happen that night.

"Call us in the morning when you want to come home," Mom said.

"Yes." Val would be so happy to call in the morning when it would, in one way or another, be over. She walked toward the lobby and then stopped. She gripped the handle of the canvas bag so tightly that her fingernails dug into her palms. It took all her courage to stand there as she watched her family get swallowed by the night.

Thirty-four

M au stretched. She felt each vertebra shift back into its proper place, like a chromatic scale on a Steinway grand. She hopped up onto the windowsill. She curled into a ball without knocking over any of the statues and stroked her fur with her tongue. She did not neglect the tip of her tail. After these rituals had been performed to her satisfaction, she was ready. The sounds of the city in the distance only made the shop seem quieter. The clock ticked. The Captain snored gently as he dozed in his chair. She closed her eyes. Tonight of all nights, she needed to commune with the universe.

And then she heard a scratching noise.

Who was disturbing her? Mau opened one eye. It was early for mice, but if they wanted to meet Mau sooner, she was happy to oblige.

Her nostrils quivered. No, not mice. Human. Tasman,

to be specific. He wasn't near the food, so she shut her eye—but only for a moment. Curiosity got the better of her. She had to see what he was doing.

She crept down off the windowsill and padded softly between the aisles, past the sleeping Captain, past the glass cases where the Captain displayed his more valuable items. The shop was dark, but she could see Tasman bent over a wooden crate. He was using a metal stick to cut through the tape. Then he poked at the corner.

Mau sat down. It amused her to watch Tasman. Humans were so proud of the tools they had created. Cats, however, came equipped with everything they needed to survive. Mau licked her paw, carefully extending her sharp claws, as if to say, Now these are worth admiring.

Tasman was too busy to notice. After he removed the staples from each end of the crate, he carefully placed the slat on the floor. He felt through the small gap. Whatever he touched pleased him. He smiled and whispered, "Yes."

He quickly got to work on the second slat. He was excited now. His movements were not as deliberate. His breathing was louder.

Mau sighed. He was making a mistake. Humans often did. The closer they got to their prey, the less they could control themselves. She took a step closer, as if to lend him her own powers of concentration. As if she knew what he was after.

But Tasman ignored her. He was in such a hurry to remove the second slat that he let it drop to the floor. He reached into the crate.

The lights blazed on. The Captain's voice shouted, "I got a gun!"

Tasman wasn't as clever as a mouse. He didn't scurry away. He took something wrapped in cloth from inside the crate.

The Captain lurched along the aisles until he saw Tasman. "You!" He slammed the antiquated pistol on top of a display case. "Didn't think you'd be stealing from me again. Did you want another present for that girl?"

Tasman stood taller. "I'm not stealing. It's mine."

The Captain saw what Tasman was unwrapping. "So you found it."

Tasman held the earthenware bowl closer to his face. He blew gently into it. Scraps of straw floated on his breath and then drifted to the ground. He slowly twisted the bowl in his hand, following the spiral of words that led to its center. No matter which way he turned the bowl, the demon with its rock teeth and unbalanced eyes grinned up at him defiantly.

"How did you know where it was?" the Captain said.

"The box was labeled in my grandfather's handwriting."

The Captain picked up a piece of the crate. "How do you know?"

"I read his journal entries. I read how he found the bowl in Nippur, Iraq."

"He had to write things like that to establish a provenance. Had to have a paper trail for the collectors. The bowl could still be a fake—even if it's a very old fake."

Tasman hugged the bowl against his chest. "He didn't think so. He believed in its powers."

"Bah." The Captain threw down the slat and lumbered over to sit in his chair. "I should have sold it when I had the chance."

"Why don't you want me to have it?"

"I don't want you to be like all those superstitious fools. Of course I shouldn't complain about them. They've kept us in business for years. Why just the other day I got a letter from a lady. Let's see. Where did I put that? I want to show you. You'll get a chuckle." The Captain pawed through some papers on his desk.

"I'm going to take the bowl," Tasman said.

The Captain stood up again. "You can't do that. It's dangerous."

"How can it be dangerous if it's just an old bowl?"

The two stared at each other.

"Why do you want the bowl anyway?" the Captain said.

"To bind the demons," Tasman whispered.

Val counted to two hundred. Twice. Then she counted fifty more. The lights of the lobby only emphasized the obvious. The dark was getting darker. She couldn't wait any longer. She had to go whether or not Tasman showed up. Too much depended on it. She picked up the bag and went outside.

She walked slowly toward the park. She froze when she heard footsteps running behind her.

A jogger passed by.

Val watched the bounce of the girl's orange shoes. She set her shoulders and walked on. She didn't look right or left. She couldn't worry that something had happened to Tasman. Or that she wouldn't know what to do without him. Worrying wouldn't help. She was all by herself in front of the goal, defending a penalty kick. Her arms could only reach so far. Her legs could only jump so high. She didn't know where the kick would come. None of that mattered. She would hurl herself across the goal. And if she failed, at least she would know she had tried.

Then someone came up behind her and grabbed the handle of the canvas bag.

Val tugged back and stuck out her foot to trip the thief.

Tasman sprawled at her feet.

"Oh, no!" Val said.

"I'm okay." Tasman gingerly felt whatever was inside his battered backpack. He sighed with relief. "Everything is okay."

He got to his feet.

"I'm so sorry. I didn't know it was you," Val said.

"I was so late, I was running to catch up. I thought I should help you." He took the canvas shopping bag.

She was glad he didn't grab her sleeping bag or her pillow. That would have been weird—even though the pillowcase was clean so it didn't have any slobber spots.

"You have a lot of baggage. I don't mean the emotional kind. You have very little of that. You seem to be traveling down the interstate of life without carrying any cargo. You lack even the burden of being grateful you have no burden."

"You talk more when you're nervous," Val said.

"You're right. Now my baggage is different from yours. I have very few actual objects. Instead I carry my history, my knowledge of my history, and my efforts to rationalize my knowledge of my history. And since I can't, I can try to mitigate." He spread the fingers of one hand over the round shape protruding from his backpack.

"What's 'mitigate'?"

"To ameliorate."

She rolled her eyes at him.

"Sorry. To make it better."

She placed her hand on the backpack, too. "So you got the bowl."

"Yes."

"Was the Captain mad? Are you in trouble?"

"I don't care. I had to have it. Look at the world we live in." He pointed to the enormous colorful orbs that seemed to float inside the Museum of Natural History. "An evil mischief maker has imprisoned some moons inside that gigantic box."

She smiled and pointed to the shadowy trees that hovered above the dark gray wall. "And there? What about there?"

He stopped. He had nothing to say about the park.

The sun had set. The city streets were brightly lit. The distant buildings glowed. The path they must take, however, was marked by only a few flickering globes.

They stopped when they reached the wall.

"We could go in the entrance," Val said

"We could read abridged books. We could drink decaffeinated coffee. We could listen to Muzak versions of Beatles songs." Tasman put the bag on top of the wall and climbed up, taking care not to bump his backpack against the stones.

Val threw the sleeping bag over and joined him on top of the wall. They stood side by side. And then, without saying a word, they jumped down into the darkness of the park.

The city sounds faded as they followed the curve of the path. He was silent, as if listening for something in the dark. The squish of her shoes. The jingle of her backpack. The sound of her breathing. The sound of his breathing. They came to the theater where Shakespeare plays were performed in the summer. He paused to stare at a statue of Romeo and Juliet embracing.

"Is something wrong?" Val said.

"No, no. I just was wondering." He glanced at Val, and then back at the statue, and then at Val again.

"What?"

He lifted the bag higher. "Might there be food in here?"

"I guess you don't know my mom. Are you hungry?"

"Always. You should be, too. Hungry for knowledge, hungry for justice, hungry for truth, hungry for . . ." he paused.

"Cookies?" she suggested.

"Yes."

"Come on." She led the way. Just past the entrance to the theater, a pier jutted out into a small pond. He put down the bag and sat on a bench. She got out a large plastic container and offered it to him.

He selected a cookie and devoured it in three bites. "These are good."

"And good for you."

"I can tell."

He smiled at her. She wasn't used to his silence. It was unsettling. She looked across the pond, where the tall castle rose up from the great rocks. Lanora loved to have adventures there. She was never a princess who dwelled within. She was the leader of the Mongolian hordes who stormed the ramparts and conquered it all.

Val wondered where Lanora was at that moment. Was she packing for her trip tomorrow? What would she think about what Val and Tasman were doing? What *were* they doing? They shouldn't be sitting there, in the near darkness, at the edge of someone else's fairy tale.

"Let's go, okay?" She stood up.

"Wait." He pulled her back to the bench.

She landed clumsily on his leg. She quickly slid off.

"Can I have another cookie?" he whispered.

She offered him the container again. He took two. He ate more slowly than she had ever seen any kid eat. He was acting so unlike himself, she wished she could see his eyes. Maybe then she would know why he was lingering on the bench. Was there something he wanted to say? "Is something wrong?" she said.

"No. Why do you ask?"

"You're acting so weird. I mean, you usually do. But now you're acting different."

"You mean normal?" He slipped out from the straps of the backpack and carefully placed it on the bench beside him. He touched the shape briefly. Then he turned toward her. She could feel him thinking something so intensely; she could almost hear the gears grinding in his skull. Suddenly she knew what that was. "It's not going to work, is it?"

"What?"

"That's what you're trying *not* to tell me. The ceremony isn't going to work. We're wasting our time. Lanora is doomed."

He shook his head. "I wasn't thinking about Lanora."

"Isn't that why we're here?"

He took hold of her hand and squeezed her fingers. His skin wasn't soft.

She couldn't untangle all the emotions in the air. The dread. The dark. The distant glow of the city. The glitter of the skyscrapers in the distance. The fairy-tale castle above the dark lagoon. The future wasn't as far away as she thought.

She heard something rustling in the bushes. She glanced

over her shoulder and then turned back to see if he had
heard it, too.

"Taz?" she said.

He smiled. "I have achieved Taz."

He leaned in to kiss her.

Thirty-five

Lanora pushed a few leaves out of the way so she could see. Were they really kissing? Was Val letting her lips touch a boy's lips? Was Tasman choosing Val as the recipient of his kiss? Yes. Yes. Yes. Here it was—this most momentous of moments. Lanora was so excited.

Then she remembered. This was Val's kiss. The moment from which there could be no return belonged to Val.

Lanora shut her eyes. Watching other people kiss was the worst. No, the worst was watching when you wanted to be kissing. When you desperately wanted something good to happen to you, but instead you got a front-row seat for someone else's happiness.

Now she was sorry she had followed them. Now it seemed like she had chosen another wrong path. Another road to misery. Why had she been curious? Why had she even gone into the park? Why had she wanted to say good-bye to the Bower? She groaned a little. Then she covered her mouth.

They stopped kissing and turned to look toward Lanora's hiding place.

Lanora held her breath. There was something worse than watching people kiss—being caught in the act of watching people kiss.

"We should get going," Tasman said.

"Yes," Val said.

They kissed again. This time their lips touched in a different way. This time they seemed to claim courage from each other.

Val shouldered the sleeping bag and the pillow. Tasman slid his arms through the straps of his backpack and picked up the canvas bag. Then they joined hands and walked deeper into the park.

Lanora was shocked. Where did they think they were going? Deeper meant darker. And darker meant that anything could happen—most likely any bad thing. She decided to go back home. Her mom would be so upset if she discovered Lanora had snuck down the fire escape. But Lanora couldn't leave her hiding place yet.

Tasman and Val had stopped in front of a statue of a king riding into battle. The king held two crossed swords high in the air, one in each hand.

"Did you bring a sword?" Val said.

Tasman hit himself on the head like he was an idiot. "Oh, gee. I completely forgot."

"We'll have to save Lanora without one," Val said.

Had Lanora really heard Val say that? Val had to be kidding. But she had sounded so serious. Like she really did want to save Lanora.

Val and Tasman took the left fork of the path and continued on into the park.

Lanora came out from the bushes. The wind tossed her hair, along with the branches of that tree. She twisted her hair with her hand to bring it under control. Why would they want to save her? She wanted to laugh. Save her? Yeah, right. She dared them to. She wondered just how they thought they could do that. What kind of crazy scheme had they invented?

She stopped in front of the king with his crossed swords. Nobody saved anybody anymore. That was ancient history.

And yet she, too, took the left fork and went deeper into the park.

A tall, narrow prism of gray stone rose up above the tops of the trees and pointed toward the sky.

"The obelisk," Tasman whispered.

Val squeezed Tasman's hand.

The path curved through the woods. They lost site of the towering stone. Then there it was again, in a small plaza surrounded by groves of short trees and bushes. They climbed twelve steps and stopped. The obelisk was much bigger than she had expected.

In the center of the plaza was a large base about four feet high. On top of it was a massive cement cube. On top of that, much higher than Val could reach, four fierce metal crabs were ready to attack. The obelisk balanced uneasily on their backs.

The obelisk had been carved from one huge piece of granite. As Val's eyes traveled up and up along its sides, it seemed to lean ominously toward her. She moved closer to Tasman, who was studying one of the plaques between the railing and the monument.

"'The Horus, Strong-Bull-Beloved-of-Ra. There is no-one who did what he did, in the house of his father.'"

"What are you reading?" Val said.

"A translation of what the Egyptians inscribed in the granite."

Val could barely see the strange markings carved in each side of the stone.

"Most of the hieroglyphics have been worn away." Tasman raised his hands above his head, up toward the stone. "And so we'll never know what Horus did, in the house of his father."

Val raised her arms, as well. Her hands trembled. Tasman was close to her. She felt her heart pound. Something was going to happen, she thought. Here. Now. The clouds wheeled around the pointed tip of the obelisk. It seemed to hold up the entire sky.

"Horus was the son of Ra. Sons have always inherited from their fathers. Sometimes it's a kingdom. And sometimes . . ."

"Sometimes?" Val said.

"Sometimes it isn't." He lowered his arms and took off his backpack to set it on the ground. He looked at the plaza. He pounded the bricks with his fists.

"What's wrong?" Val touched his shoulder.

"We can't do the ceremony!" Tasman grabbed her arms.

"Why not?"

"It won't be safe. We can't bury the bowl."

Val rubbed the cracks between the bricks. Just a little grit came up. It would be impossible to dig a hole. She looked at the grove of short trees that surrounded the plaza. "What about over there? It's near enough, isn't it?"

They held hands and walked around the edge of the plaza, trying to adjust to the idea of the dark. There were four separate groups of twisted trees, one on each side of the plaza. The groves were dense. The twisted branches made a tangle of vegetation. But there was dirt below the leaves.

"It'll be okay." Val walked into the shadows between two trees on the southern side of the plaza. She stamped on the dirt with her sneaker. "The ground is pretty hard. You didn't bring a shovel, did you?"

Tasman grabbed the backpack. "Maybe we can dig with a stick. Do you see any on the ground?" He took one tentative step into the grove.

Something rustled in the bushes.

They both ran back. They ducked under the railing and stood with their backs against the base of the obelisk. Tasman moved the backpack so that it was in front of him. Then he put his arm around Val so that he could protect them both.

There was a scuffling and a short screech.

Mau came out, carrying a small rat in her mouth. She laid the corpse at their feet.

Val looked at Tasman. "Maybe Mau cleansed the place for us?"

He shook his head. "We can't bury the bowl there."

"How about the other side?" Val pointed to a grove on the western edge of the plaza.

"You think that's the only rat in the park?" Tasman said.

Lanora was sure it was not. Even though her hiding place was on the opposite side of the obelisk, she tried to climb up a scrubby tree. If anything crawled across her feet, she knew she would scream.

Surely now Val would give up whatever she intended to do and go home.

But Val said, "We can't quit. We have to save Lanora."

Tasman shook his head. "It isn't safe."

"You have the bowl. It's kind of buried in your backpack. It'll be okay. Come on. Get out the first thing." Val tried to open up his backpack.

He held it close to himself. His breathing was so ragged, Lanora wondered if he had asthma. Then she realized he was afraid. He was very, very afraid. Again she wondered, Just what were they about to do? The night felt potent. Lanora had no idea what had charged the atmosphere. There were so many mysteries. She wished Tasman had read more of the translation of what had been carved in the obelisk. Then she shook her head. What could some ancient symbols from the Middle East possibly mean to her?

Val touched Tasman's arm.

Tasman nodded.

The clouds fell away from the moon. The pale gray obelisk seemed to float against the dark sky. Lanora gripped the branches more tightly. She hoped that their trembling wouldn't give her away.

Tasman reached into his backpack and handed Val a clump of feathers.

Val held them up toward the obelisk. The feathers spun in a slow circle.

"Mercury's ankle wings," Lanora whispered.

Val solemnly walked toward the obelisk.

Lanora muttered under her breath, "Oh, Mercury, travel fast through the dark."

Val reached over the railing and placed the ankle wings on the narrow ledge of the westernmost side of the cube. Then she walked to her backpack and unzipped it.

"Wait. You have to say something," Tasman whispered.

"But I don't know what to say," Val whispered.

A loud groaning came from the eastern side of the plaza.

Thirty-six

Four people in dark robes emerged from the bushes on the eastern side. They spoke in muffled voices as they walked around the obelisk. Their footsteps marked the rhythm of the syllables.

"Do not forget."

"Why you are here."

"Do not forget."

"Your purpose tonight."

"Do not forget."

"The words."

"The words."

"The words."

"The words."

The figures stopped and stood in a row in front of the obelisk. Now that they were closer, Lanora recognized Gillian, Tina, Olivia, and Helena.

"What are you guys doing here?" Val said.

"You invited us," Gillian said.

"Besides, you obviously need our help," Tina said.

"Words are our specialty," Olivia said.

"The words possess the meaning. Without them, you have just a few fake feathers," Helena said.

"They're right. If you don't use the proper language, you might get unintended consequences," Tasman said.

Helena came closer to stare at Tasman. "Might you be the one who wrote the mysterious marks on the sidewalk?"

Tasman nodded.

"It is an honor to meet someone who knows the ancient symbols."

The poets bowed to Tasman and stepped back.

Helena waved her hand. "Please. Try again."

"But I don't know what to say," Val said.

"What consequences do you intend?" Helena said.

Lanora nearly blurted out, "She wants to save me!"

"Okay." Val held up the feathers. "This is supposed to be a gift—"

Gillian interrupted her. "Wait. Don't explain here. You're too near the ceremonial spot."

The poets surrounded Val.

"Come with us, a slight distance away." Olivia smoothed Val's golden hair.

"But." Val looked over their shoulders at Tasman, who stood clutching the backpack.

"We will return when we have found the words for your meaning," Helena said.

"Come on, Tasman," Val said.

"It's okay," Tasman said.

As soon as they disappeared around the eastern edge of the plaza, Tasman opened the backpack and took out something.

Lanora moved carefully so that she could see what he held in his hands. It seemed to be an ordinary brown bowl, like the ones vegans used for their wholesome meals.

Tasman held it close to his chest. He sighed.

Lanora echoed his sigh.

He quickly turned toward her and held the bowl out in her direction. She wanted to reassure him. But his face was so frightened, she didn't know if she could. How could she tell him that it was going to be okay? Wasn't she equally alone in the dark, uncertain and afraid?

Luckily, at that moment, Val called from the shadows. "We're ready."

Tasman put the bowl away and zipped shut his backpack.

The girls returned. Val held a notebook close to her, squinting at the page as she mumbled whatever had been written there.

Helena shut the notebook and took it away. "Speak from your heart."

Val nodded. She stood next to Tasman on the southern side of the obelisk. The poets stood in a line along the steps at the western side. Mau appeared on top of the base, between two of the fierce crabs. No one knew how she had jumped so high. She sat just as Bastets always sat in their temples long ago in ancient Egypt.

"Now?" Val said.

Clouds massed in the sky. The dark only got darker. Wait, Lanora thought. Wait until the moon returns. But they might have to be there until sunrise brought them more light.

Val coughed a little to clear her throat. Then she raised the ankle wings high above her head.

"I give this offering to speed the messenger's way. Make haste so that our work can be done."

Val walked counterclockwise all the way around the obelisk. She knelt to place the ankle wings at the southeast corner.

"Make haste," Tasman said.

"Make haste," the poets echoed.

"Make haste," Lanora muttered.

Val took something from her backpack. Lanora couldn't see what it was, even after Tasman brought a lit match close to Val's hand. A foul smoke rose up. The stench was familiar. But Lanora thought she was mistaken. How on earth could Val have gotten one of her father's cigars?

Val waved the cigar as she walked around the obelisk, knocking ashes at each of the four corners.

"I offer this gift from the Star Tamer. It symbolizes his power and his willingness to use that power for salvation."

"Salvation," Tasman and the poets echoed.

Lanora shook her head. Her father didn't care about her salvation. He only wanted to send her away.

Val stubbed out the cigar and placed it at the northwest corner.

The fire was out, but the odor lingered like a memory. Lanora could almost hear her father telling her that she had a choice. She didn't have to go to Greywacke. But if she didn't go there, then what would she do instead? She glanced up at the obelisk. The gray rock was silent. Why were those messages carved in inscrutable hieroglyphics? Why had they been worn away by time?

Val took something else from the backpack. She held up a red ribbon. A shiny disk dangled from its end. "I give my treasure, from my heart. So that she might be soothed by the ministering winds."

"Be soothed," Tasman and the poets echoed.

Val moved her arm as she circled the plaza. The golden disk swung out, away from the tall tower of stone.

Lanora wondered why it flashed in stark contrast to the shadows. It was just a little bit of reflected light. It shouldn't be able to shine. Unless there was such a thing as magic.

There wasn't, of course. Not here. Not now. Not with that dead rat on the plaza and who knew how many live ones crawling around. Nobody really believed in magic anymore—and yet there was a towering stone inscribed with symbols that hadn't entirely worn away. There was a wisp of smoke that had conjured up a blessing from her father. There was the beautiful concentration on Val's face.

At that moment, the curtain of clouds fell away from the moon.

Could there be magic? If there was such a thing, then Lanora might have a friend in a soccer shirt. And that friend could have friends who could command the power of words and weren't afraid to be seen wearing dark robes. And another friend whose ideas were as wild as his hair. If there was magic, then those people could care about someone who had lost her way.

Val kept swinging the red ribbon and the shiny disk. Lanora recognized it now. It wasn't real metal; it was plastic. And yet Lanora knew it was more precious than gold. She had never been so proud and happy as when her best friend Val had won that medal for Most Valuable Player.

That had been magic. And so was this moment. The beauty of these words, these deeds, and these people was so intense that Lanora shivered. She began to believe that she might be saved.

A man burst from the dark grove at the southern edge.

He stumbled onto the plaza with his arms stretched out in front of him. "Got-got-got get-get-get," he stuttered as he rushed toward Val.

"Look out!" the poets shrieked.

Val turned around quickly.

But it was too late. The man reached around Val's neck to grab the gold.

Thirty-seven

Val couldn't see the man. He had rushed out of the dark. He had come from nowhere. No—not from nowhere. He had come from a place of misery and madness. Their ceremony had opened a door and let out this demon.

The man's arm pressed against Val's neck. She felt his body jerk as he tried to catch the spinning disk. His ropes of hair struck her face. His breath burned her skin.

"Got-got-got get-get-get go-go-gold." His flailing hand only knocked the disk farther from him.

Val tried to wriggle free, but his grip on her neck was surprisingly strong.

"Give it to me! I see you, nasty rats. That's my gold. Mine."

She tried to give him the medal, but his arm was twisted around hers. The ribbon was tangled in her fingers. "Take it," she said. But her voice was hoarse and could hardly be heard.

"Take it," the poets pleaded.

Their frightened faces seemed to float in the shadows above their dark robes.

Where was Tasman? Was he still there? Had he run to get help? Or had he just run? She remembered all the times he had been so afraid. And now she realized that he had been right. They should never have come to the park tonight. How could he have thought he could be protected by an old bowl? Even if they had buried it.

Val tried to turn toward the place where she had last seen Tasman. But the man pushed her back the other way.

Mau slunk toward the man, growling from deep inside her body.

The man barked like a dog. "What good are you, Bastet?"

Mau yowled.

"You're a false god! We worshiped you in the shadow of the pyramids. And you let the vermin get our gold."

The man kicked at Mau. Mau hissed and spat. The man's boot struck her body. She yowled in pain as she seemed to fly across the plaza and into the shadows.

Val stared at the man's feet. He was wearing blue boots— exactly like the ones Tasman used to wear. This was the man who had come into the park the day Tasman gave her the amulet. She had seen the man again in the line for the soup kitchen. She recognized his blue robes. But why did he have Tasman's boots?

The man finally got hold of the medal. "Gold!" he cried. He brought it to his mouth and bit it. He spat.

"Worthless!" He flung the medal into the bushes.

"Sorry," Val whispered. She thought he would let her go. But he tightened his grip on her neck.

He pulled the pink wand from his belt. He pressed the point of the star against her cheek. "You got your gold hidden."

Val shook her head.

"Don't try to trick me."

"She doesn't have gold," Helena said.

"Sure she does. Look at her. Look." The man touched Val's yellow hair. He lifted up a few strands and watched them fall from his fingers.

"It's just hair," Helena said.

"It's gold," the man hissed. "Gold."

He started to drag Val with him. Then the medal came flying back from the bushes. It hit his back. He stopped.

Someone stepped from the shadows.

Lanora had waited for someone else to do something. Let Tasman save Val. Wasn't he Val's boyfriend? Lanora could see him crouching down behind the base of the obelisk, hiding from the madness. His eyes shut tight. His hands clutching the brown bowl. He was overwhelmed by the situation. He couldn't help. And those other girls in their black robes. There were four of them, but they were frightened, too. They had never faced something that belonged in the dark.

But Lanora had.

When the disk landed in the dirt by her feet, she picked it up. It was still wet from where the man had bit it. She dropped it. Then she saw the man dragging Val toward the shadows. There was no time to think. Lanora picked up the medal again and flung it. Somehow or other—magically, miraculously—the disk hit the man. It didn't hurt him. But he stopped.

Lanora came out from the grove of trees and walked slowly toward the obelisk.

Everyone stared at her.

Val whispered, "Lanora?"

"Lanora, Lanora, Lanora," the man chanted in his sing-song voice. He stared at her, but he kept the point of the star pressing into Val's cheek.

Lanora kept walking, slowly, placing one foot directly in front of the other. She felt like she was crossing a great canyon on a thin rope. Don't look down, she warned herself. If she thought about what would happen to Val if Lanora took the wrong step, then she would most certainly crash at the bottom. She had to keep walking and hope that she could find the right things to say.

But what were the right things? What good were words? She thought of all the things people said to her. Why did people say, "Feel better"? Why didn't they know the darkness was all around?

"Why?" she blurted out.

"Why? Why ask why? There is no why. There is no reason. There's rhyme. Not reason. Rhyme and time and crime." He waved his pink wand as if he were conducting a symphony. Val tried to slip away. He tightened his grip and pressed the point of the pink star against Val's neck.

"Why do you want gold?" Lanora said.

"Got-got-got get-get-get go-go-gold," the man stuttered.

"What will you do when you get some? What will you buy?" Lanora took another step.

"Buy? Nothing! Can't go in a store. Shut me out. Kick me out. That's why I have to have gold. Gold gives me peace. Gold fills my mind. Gold makes the light."

"Did you used to have it?" Lanora was closer now. She could see the man's eyes.

He leaned toward her to whisper. "The vermin nibbled it away."

"That happened to me, too," Lanora said.

"What kind of vermin you got?" the man said.

"Mice," Lanora said.

"Mice? That's nothing. I got devils. I got demons. They

fly around my head. What can you do with demons?" the man said.

"We have a bowl," Val said.

"A bowl hole troll stole," the man chanted.

"An incantation bowl," Val said.

The man stopped. He turned Val so that he could see her face. "Where is it?"

Val hesitated, unsure of what to say.

"I saw that bowl. It's over there. In the grove. You'd better go get it." Lanora pointed in the direction from where the man had come.

The man took a step. Then he stopped. He couldn't be tricked. "I been there. I didn't see a bowl. Besides. Don't want the bowl. Want gold."

Then from a different part of the darkness, they heard a halting voice trying to speak. Or was it just the wind?

"Shhh," the man said. He put the wand to his ear to listen.

"You are bound and sealed, all you . . . demons and devils. . . . By that powerful bond. . . ."

The man dragged Val toward the voice. Tasman came out of the eastern grove. He held the bowl against his chest.

"Who's that? Who's there?"

Tasman stopped just at the edge of the darkness.

The man squinted at Tasman. "Why do you have a bowl?"

Tasman held the bowl so that the opening was pointed toward the man. As he extended his arms, they trembled so much he seemed about to drop the bowl. But he clung to it.

The man released Val. The wand clattered to the bricks. He came closer and closer. Tasman tensed, but he didn't back away. The man pointed at the drawing of the demon at the bottom of the bowl. Then he took several steps back and hid his finger inside his robe. He squinted at Tasman. "Where did you get it?"

"My grandfather found it in the desert, near Nippur, Iraq," Tasman said.

"Your grandfather? No! Not your grandfather. My father. This is what my father found," the man said.

"Your father. My grandfather," Tasman said.

The man nodded. "Tasman."

"Yes," Tasman said.

"No," the poets murmured.

The man stared into the bowl. He moved his head in a circle so that his eyes followed the spiral of words until they descended to the demon at the center.

Then he yelped. The poets gasped.

"Why do you have it?" the man said.

"To bind the demons," Tasman said.

The man laughed. He spun around and around.

"Stop," Lanora said.

The man stopped.

"We need to finish our ceremony," Lanora said.

The man shook his head. "Why? Would it help? Nothing helps. Nothing except gold. Got-got-got get-get-get go-go-gold." He tried to grab Val again.

Lanora rushed over to stand between them. She looked the man in the eyes. "Maybe you didn't do it right."

"Right right, wrong or right," the man sang.

"Maybe you didn't have enough people." Val stood beside Lanora.

"Maybe you forgot some of the words," Helena said.

"Maybe you were too loud," Tina said.

"Maybe you were too clever," Gillian said

"Maybe you didn't speak from the heart," Olivia said.

When they had all formed a circle around the man, Lanora said, "You'd better try again. Come on, Tasman."

"Tas man, has plan, raz fan, jazz can," the man said.

As he spewed his nonsense, Tasman slowly walked toward them. He hugged the bowl to his chest. He placed his cheek against its smooth surface. Then he sighed deeply. He held out the bowl. One by one, they all put their hands on its rim. Together they lifted it above the man's head.

"You are bound and sealed." Tasman's voice was hesitant at first. "All you demons and devils. By that powerful bond."

"No," Lanora said. "By *this* powerful bond."

Tasman looked at the man. The man tilted his head so that his hair fell away from his eyes. They stared at each other. Then they said together, "By *this* powerful bond."

"You evil one," the man shouted, "who causes the hearts of men to go astray, and appears in the dream of the night, and in the vision of the day."

"You are conquered and sealed," Tasman shouted, too.

"You demons and devils are trapped by this incantation in this bowl."

The wind swept away the words and brought back a whisper from the trees. Then the bowl slowly began to rotate on the tips of their outstretched fingers.

Mau circled around their legs in the opposite direction.

The bowl stopped moving.

Mau cried out once. The clouds parted. The girls all let go of the bowl. Tasman and the man slowly lowered it all the way to the ground.

It sat on the plaza, upside down. The demons trapped underneath.

"Vanquished are the black arts," the man said quietly.

"Vanquished are the mighty spells," Tasman said.

"Tasman," the man said.

Tasman nodded.

"Son," the man said.

"Yes," Tasman said.

"I'm sorry. Sorry I can't be. Sorry I'm not."

"It's okay," Tasman said. "I'm okay." Tasman picked up the bowl. He took a deep breath. Then he handed it to the man. "Take it."

The man blinked.

"Take the bowl. Bury it by the place where you dwell."

The man sniffed the bowl. Then he raised it up above his head. He walked slowly down the stairs at the western edge of the plaza and disappeared into the night.

Thirty-eight

No one moved. The powerful bond held them. No one spoke. Not even the poets had words to describe what had happened—or what could happen next.

Then, from somewhere in the darker part of the park, they heard barking. They assumed it was a dog—until Mau, who wasn't afraid of anything, dashed away from the obelisk.

The spell had been broken. They all ran after the streak of black cat. They didn't stop to pick up the backpacks or the bag of food. They hurried away from the obelisk and the shadows, through tangled bushes, toward a large building on the eastern edge of the park. None of them recognized the Metropolitan Museum of Art from the back. Just north of the building, they discovered a neatly mowed lawn. They flung themselves onto the carpet of grass. The girls all sprawled close to one another. Tasman sat off by himself, with his head down and his arms locked around his knees.

They breathed deeply, as if for the first time since the man had grabbed Val by the neck.

Val sat up and coughed a little.

"Are you all right?" Lanora said.

The girls raised their heads to look at Val. Tasman shifted his position so he could see beneath his arm.

"Yes. I was just wondering. How will we get home?" Val said.

Lanora fell back onto the grass. She wasn't ready to start thinking about any aspect of the future, however near or far.

"That is the question," Helena said.

"How to return?" Gillian said.

"Can we return?" Olivia said.

"Go back in time?" Tina said.

"No," Val said.

"She's right. We can't undo what has been done. We have seen what we have seen, heard what we heard. The neurons of our brains have been irrevocably altered. It's foolish to pretend that we can forget the unforgettable, to return to a safe place. Why even try?" Tasman said.

"I mean," Val interrupted him, "are we walking or taking the bus?"

The poets laughed. Helena hugged Val. "What would we do without our practical Val?"

"Does anyone have any money they could lend me?" Val said. "My metro card is in my backpack."

"We could go get it," Lanora said.

They all looked toward the park and quickly turned away. No one wanted to go back into that tangle of darkness—no matter how powerful the incantation had been.

"I guess we're walking." Val jumped to her feet.

The others were slower to rise. Tasman didn't move at all.

Mau walked over to the building and sat on a ledge. Just barely visible beyond a wall of glass were limestone bricks and columns. An entire temple had been reconstructed inside this special wing of the museum.

"The Temple of Dendur," Helena said.

"Who's Dendur?" Olivia said.

"Did he endure?" Gillian said.

"Or did he donate a lot of money to the museum?" Tina said.

"Dendur is a place. Or *was* a place." Tasman pulled up tufts of grass and let them fall away from his hands.

"What happened?" Olivia was saddened by even the loss of an ancient city.

"They built the Aswan Dam. Dendur was overwhelmed by the waters of the mighty Nile. The Egyptians gave us this temple to thank us for saving some other temples from that man-made flood," Tasman said.

Lanora felt Val look at her, like there was something she wanted to say. Lanora didn't want a speech of gratitude. She wouldn't have known how to respond. She got up and walked toward the street.

Val followed. "Is it shorter if we go north or south?"

Val smiled. Lanora smiled back. Because of course Val knew that Lanora would know the answer to this question. That was what was good about an old friend.

"The top of the park is twenty-nine blocks from here. The bottom is twenty-two," Lanora said.

"She has not only saved Val, she has saved us fourteen blocks," Tina said.

The poets joined Val and Lanora at the edge of Fifth Avenue. Tasman hadn't moved. Lanora wondered why Val didn't go get him. But maybe Val couldn't. So many things had happened after that kiss.

"Aren't you coming, Tasman?" Helena called.

"It's going to be a long walk," Gillian said.

"We'll need the distraction of your knowledge of arcane architecture," Tina said.

Tasman jumped up and ran past Val to walk with the poets. "Are you only interested in arcane architecture? Or will any alliteration do? How about archaic architecture?"

Tasman pointed to the massive stone steps leading up to the museum.

"But it isn't useless. When the museum is open, the stairs are a destination," Helena said.

No one sat there now. The sidewalk was deserted. A city bus stopped and waited, but they had to wave it away.

"Forty-four blocks plus the ones across the bottom of the park," Olivia said.

"An epic journey," Helena said.

"An Odyssey," Gillian said.

"With Sirens," Tina said, as the sounds of a distant ambulance wailed.

"Lash me to the mast," Helena said.

"Ulysses was wrong to want to hear the singing of the maidens. He risked too much, and for what? Hearing that music probably drove him crazy because he knew he could never actually enjoy it," Tasman said.

"Why not?" Val said.

"The ship sails on by." Tasman ran ahead of them all.

Lanora walked silently beside Val. They were passing one of the places in the park where they used to play when they were little. Just over the wall was the pond where Stuart Little had bravely steered the toy boat to victory. Next to the pond were two statues. One was of Alice sitting on the magic mushroom. The other was of Hans Christian

Andersen reading to the ugly duckling to let her know she would be beautiful in the end.

"So how did you get a cigar from my father?" Lanora said.

Val shrugged. "I asked him for it."

"You're kidding." Lanora couldn't believe it was that simple.

"Well, it was hard to get in to see him. But once I got past the guards, he was pretty cool."

"Wow." Lanora thought about this as she looked up and up and up at the buildings that bordered the park. Their glitter defied the night sky.

"Did he talk to you?" Val said.

Lanora nodded. "He said I don't have to go to Greywacke Academy if I don't want to."

"So you won't be going away tomorrow? That's great!" Val hugged her.

Lanora stopped walking. "I don't know. I can't just go back to M.S. 10. So much has happened."

The poets returned to where Lanora and Val stood.

"I guess it would be hard to go back," Val said.

"So don't," Helena said.

"Don't?" Val said.

"Go forward." Gillian pointed with her arm.

"Go sideways." Tina sashayed toward the curb.

"Go up." Olivia climbed on a park bench.

The rest of the poets joined her. They pulled Lanora up with them. They laughed. They clung together even after they jumped down. It felt good to be surrounded by their silky robes as they continued on their way.

"Hey, I've fallen a little behind in math," Lanora said to Helena.

"You're still way ahead of the rest," Helena said. "But you can count upon me for whatever help I can give."

"*Count* on you?" Lanora said.

"I think you'll be a fine *addition* to our club," Gillian said.

"The missing *variable*," Tina said.

Up ahead, Val was walking with Tasman. They were not holding hands. Their conversation was hushed until Val said, "But nothing bad really happened. Lanora saved me."

"Yes. *Lanora* saved you." Tasman ran down the sidewalk as best he could in his old snow boots.

"You save me, too," Val called after him.

Finally they reached the southeast corner of the park. The end of the wilderness. They paused to admire the glitter of the tall buildings, the fountain with tiers like a wedding cake, a row of horses with carriages fit for royalty, and a brightly lit rococo building.

"Look! It's the Plaza Hotel!" Helena cried.

"Eloise!" Olivia said.

"Eloise?" Tasman said.

"The girl who lived in the Plaza. Who dined on room service. Who terrorized the grown-ups. Who had a turtle named Skipperdee. How could you not know Eloise?" Lanora was shocked.

"The Captain's library doesn't have much in the way of contemporary literature," Tasman said.

"What kinds of books does it have?" Olivia said.

"Is that where you found *The Book of Dares*?" Helena said.

"No." Tasman walked over to stand next to the fountain.

"I have misspoken," Helena said.

"Misspoke," Gillian said.

Lanora waited to see if Val would go talk to him. But Val was kicking a rock across the sidewalk. So Lanora went to put her foot on the rim of the fountain, next to Tasman's snow boot.

He brushed a leaf off of his snow boot. The leaf fell into the water. It floated—for now. But a tattered leaf wasn't meant to be a boat.

"Did you come to make a wish?" Lanora said.

"My pockets, alas, are empty. If I picked up someone else's penny, that crime would undo my desires. Just like it did tonight."

"What crime did you commit?"

"The apple doesn't fall far from the tree. That expression

explains nothing, except gravity. But I think you know what I mean."

"I'm not like *my* father."

Tasman smiled. "I haven't had the pleasure of meeting the Star Tamer, but I suspect that, once you have recovered from this detour, you will return to getting what you want."

"Not just what I want."

"Don't tell me you've learned a lesson." He placed his hands to his cheek in mock amazement.

"I saw you kiss her in the park."

His hands fell helplessly to his sides.

"So you like her," Lanora said.

"Past tense would be more accurate," Tasman said.

"She likes you."

"She feels sorry for me now. And don't contradict me. It doesn't matter whether you're right or not, it's what I think."

Just at that moment, the leaf sank to the bottom. He smiled; his suspicions had been confirmed.

She pulled him around to face her. "Yes, I have learned a lesson. And this is it. That if you have a friend, you shouldn't take her for granted. You should keep that friend. No matter what. Because you've got problems and I've got problems and we've all got problems. So does Val, believe it or not—even if hers aren't as exciting as ours are."

He jerked away his arm. He needed his sleeve to wipe his nose. "This is not the era of handkerchiefs. And it isn't the era for the likes of me. I belong in the Captain's shop. With the other antiquities shipwrecked by time."

"So what are you going to do? Just stay there?"

"I have no choice. You see, I thought I could be a Taz. Sadly, I was wrong."

"You gave your father the bowl," Lanora said.

"And I already regret its loss." He leaned over and studied the money glittering at the bottom of the fountain. "So many wishes. None of them mine."

Lanora shouted back to the others. "Who has a quarter?"

The poets came closer.

"Alas, robes have no pockets," Helena said.

"Val? Do you have a quarter? A nickel? A dime?" Lanora said.

Val shook her head. "Why do you want one?"

"I need to wish," Lanora said.

Val marched over to the fountain. She leaned over the edge and scooped up a handful of coins. She offered her treasure to Lanora.

Lanora carefully selected a thin dime. She clenched it in her fist. She whispered to it. Then she tossed it into the uppermost tier of the fountain.

The poets cheered. Then they each selected a coin.

"I don't know what to wish for," Tina said.

"I always wish for three more wishes," Olivia said.

"Why not ten?" Lanora said.

"That dilutes the potency," Olivia said.

"And this is potent," Helena said, twirling around with her arms outstretched. "This has been the most astonishing of nights."

One after another, the poets flung their coins into the fountain.

Val offered the last coin to Tasman.

He shook his head. "I don't believe in wishes."

"But you believe in believing," Val said.

He looked at the coin in her outstretched hand. He touched it with his finger, to shift its position. But he didn't pick it up.

"Of course you do. How can you not?" Lanora said.

Val put her other arm around Lanora and hugged her.

"How can you not?" Lanora said again.

"You're right," he said.

He grabbed hold of Val's hand. He closed her fist around the coin. He kissed that fist. Then he stepped up onto the rim of the fountain. He raised his arms straight up into the air, and flung himself into the water.

The splash was tremendous. A multitude of tiny drops cascaded up toward the sky. And then there were more and more drops, as each girl followed Tasman's example. The laughter resounded across the plaza. It bounced off the glittering buildings and disrupted the dark corners of the park.

The sound and the light traveled farther than they knew.

A man looked up. He smiled. He wasn't sure if he had heard what he heard. But the sound was a good sound. And so he continued smoothing the dirt on top of the bowl.

Mau sat on the top of what would have been a mountain of schist. As the vibrations washed over her, the corners of her mouth curled up slightly into what would, on any other animal, be considered a smile.

She was a cat. We will never know what she was thinking. But we do know that she was very pleased with herself, as well she should be.

Acknowledgments

I'm so grateful to the Thurber House Children's Writer-in-Residence program for their generous support while I was writing this book. Staying at the Thurber House was especially inspirational because of the enthusiastic encouragement of Susanne Jaffe, Anne Touvell, Katie Poole, Erin Deel, and the intrepid Meg Brown.

I'm grateful to all readers, particularly those who took the time to write me about my earlier books. To teachers and librarians like Susan Westover, who do so much to encourage young readers. To my friends Tom and Julie Coash for their wise words and fascinating artifacts. To Rachel Berger and Kira Kelley, who read early versions and gave helpful advice. To my daughter, Sofia, who asks the best questions. To my mother, Virginia, who is a wonderful listener. To my husband, Lee, who sustains me in so many ways. To Linda Pratt, who is so much more than an agent. To everyone at Feiwel and Friends, especially my editor, Liz Szabla, whose insights and expertise made this book possible.

Finally, I'm grateful to Blackberry the cat, who graciously allowed me to stare into her green eyes.

The Book of Dares
for Lost Friends

BONUS MATERIALS

GOFISH

JANE KELLEY

© Keith Weber

What did you want to be when you grew up?
I wanted to be an actress. My child-hood seemed kind of ordinary to me. Being in plays gave me a chance to live other, more-exciting lives. I studied theater in college. After I graduated, I performed with a street theater company for many years.

When did you realize you wanted to be a writer?
When I was in my early thirties, I discovered that writing was another way to be inside of a character. Plus, as a writer, I had much more control. I could choose who that character would be. I no longer had to wait to be asked to create.

What's your most embarrassing childhood memory?
When I was in the fourth grade, a group of girls always bul-lied me on the school bus. One day, they shot spitballs at me. That was pretty humiliating—and gross. I was tired of being picked on, so I decided to throw one of their spitballs back at them. Unfortunately, the bus driver saw me. So I was the one who got yelled at, and they just laughed.

What's your favorite childhood memory?
I loved playing in the woods behind our house and on our neighborhood beach at Lake Michigan.

As a young person, who did you look up to most?
My grandmother, Katharine Carson, who was a novelist. She died when I was six. But other family members always spoke of how wise and talented she was, so sometimes, I would imagine the sort of counsel she might give me.

What was your favorite thing about school?
Spending time with my friends! I liked being in shows and playing the flute in the school band. I was a good student, but I don't recall being as excited about learning things as I am now.

What were your hobbies as a kid? What are your hobbies now?
I spent a lot of time hiking, camping, swimming, and canoeing. I played the piano, the flute, and the guitar. Being outdoors and making music are still important parts of my life. I'm in a community chorus. Singing with other people is a wonderful feeling. The group makes me sound much better than I ever would on my own.

Did you play sports as a kid?
I wasn't on any teams because I didn't believe I was athletic. When I got older, I found that I really enjoyed tennis. It's very satisfying to hit the ball hard—and keep it in the court.

What was your first job, and what was your "worst" job?
My first job was working in a factory in our basement. My father invented things in his spare time. One product was a

portable greenhouse called the Gard 'n' Gro. Our whole family assembled them and got them ready to be shipped all over the country.

My worst job was being a waitress. I had to quit after just a few weeks—I couldn't handle being nice to people who were complaining about their food.

What makes you feel better when you're sick? What do you do for your loved ones when they are sick?
When I was little, the most comforting thing was when my mother read to me and stroked my forehead. I carried on that tradition whenever my daughter was sick. And of course, I made many cups of tea and pots of soup.

What is your favorite word?
Quest. It means a journey and a search. What could be better than that? It's also part of the word "Question." And it starts with a Q, a very valuable letter indeed.

Who is your favorite fictional character?
Charlotte in *Charlotte's Web* by E. B. White. She is wonderful and wise—and she knows how to get things done.

What was your favorite book when you were a kid? Do you have a favorite book now?
Jane Eyre by Charlotte Brontë. I found it wonderfully encouraging that a smart, plain girl (who happens to be named Jane) gets love and respect in the end! Now that I'm older, I admire Marilynne Robinson's Gilead trilogy. Her writing is so beautiful. And her generous spirit is so comforting, especially when she tackles difficult topics.

What's the best advice you have ever received about writing?
Keep writing. Love the process. Find joy in what you can do each day.

What advice do you wish someone had given you when you were younger?
I wish someone had told me I didn't need to wait for permission to write. My thoughts were just as important as anyone else's. I just needed to keep working at the best way to express them.

What do you want readers to remember about your books?
My books are all very different, and yet I do return to certain themes. I write about the importance of nature, the power of believing, and the need to keep trying.

What do you consider to be your greatest accomplishment?
I have a remarkable daughter and a wonderful partnership with my husband. But Sofia and Lee had a lot to do with those successes. My own greatest accomplishment is giving voice to how someone else felt. I'm really grateful to the readers who have told me that I've done that.

Zeno is an orphaned African grey parrot.
Alya is a girl so sick, she's forgotten what it means to try.
But together, the two will discover that where
there is friendship, there is hope.

Keep reading for a sneak peek!

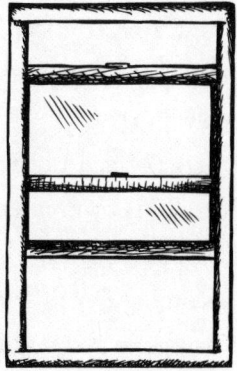

B eing outside was so exhilarating for Zeno that he got out of breath after only flying five blocks. He wasn't used to that much exercise. Of course, he had been free to fly wherever he wanted in Dr. Agard's house. However, he usually only wanted to fly the short distance between his stand and his aluminum dishes.

He perched on a tree branch and paused to look around him. The buildings in this part of Brooklyn were all very similar. They were made of brown stone, about four stories tall. Each one was squeezed against its neighbor, with a short flight of stairs between the front door and the sidewalk. The tiny front yards contained flower gardens. Tall trees arched their branches above the streets. These trees were just beginning to get their leaves. It was spring, although Zeno understood little about the seasons because the temperature was constant inside Dr. Agard's house.

A breeze ruffled his feathers. "Pfft," Zeno muttered. He would have to set them right again as soon as he found food. He was extremely hungry.

Zeno had never actually had to find his meals before. He had been fed first by his own parents, and then, after his capture, by various humans until Dr. Agard had been given the honor of becoming Zeno's servant.

Now Dr. Agard had gone away. This was not unusual. Dr. Agard took his papers and went away nearly every day. This time, Dr. Agard had left Zeno without making sure his dishes were full and Zeno had cardboard to gnaw—and without saying, "Good-bye, Zeno, you beautiful, brilliant bird."

"Booful, briyant," Zeno said. He would have to feed himself. He wasn't worried about that. For one thing, if he were in charge of finding his own food, he intended to eat only the things he liked. At the top of that list were banana-nut muffins.

"Banana nut!" Zeno squawked.

He examined the branch upon which he sat. Tiny green leaves had pushed their way up from the brown bark. Obviously this tree was not the source of the banana-nut muffins. He flew farther down the block. He saw trees with pink buds, old brown leaves, and white flowers. Where were the ones with banana-nut muffins?

He flew over a roof and perched in the branches of a pine tree that grew in the backyard between the rows of houses. From a distance, the large brown cones seemed promising, but they weren't muffins, either.

"Pffft," Zeno muttered. How could this be? Dr. Agard must have gotten the muffins from somewhere. And food grew on trees. Zeno was certain of this. Buried beneath his 127 words and sixty-three sounds was a parrot memory. It had been handed down for generations, along with the scarlet feathers of his tail and the ability to talk. Parrots found food on trees. Of course the food they found was a particular kind of palm nut that grew on a type of tree that would never survive the winter in Brooklyn. Still, Zeno felt confident that the food he craved also grew on trees. Where else could it be?

He flew on and on, trying to match the parrot memory to what he observed. Wasn't the row of buildings like a cliff? Wasn't the street with its rush of cars like a river? Wasn't the lamppost just as branchless as a palm tree?

On and on, he flew, and around and around. He didn't dare stray too far, just in case Dr. Agard came back. At any moment, Zeno expected Dr. Agard to appear, holding the white paper bag decorated with blue flowers. "So sorry to be late, old chum. Here's our Sunday treat. Banana-nut muffins!"

But that, as you know, wasn't going to happen.

"Banana nut," Zeno muttered mournfully. He flapped

down to perch on the low branch of a pear tree and bent over to preen.

The dark gray feathers that adorned his neck had gotten quite ruffled. He always found comfort in stroking his beautiful feathers. He had never been in a situation quite as stressful as this. His hunger had reached an entirely new level of emptiness. He wasn't sure what to do about that. He might have to tug at every single feather before he felt like himself again.

A high-pitched voice below him said, "Look, Mom. It's a parrot."

Zeno turned sideways to look at the human. There were two of them, both female. Neither one had the glass circles in front of their eyes like Dr. Agard did. The smaller one had spoken to Zeno. She danced around and pointed at him with a purple circle on the end of a stick.

The girl put the circle in her mouth. Was this food? Would Zeno like to eat it? He never saw shiny purple food before. He leaned closer to get a better look.

"That looks like an African grey parrot," the woman said.

Zeno bobbed his head up and down several times, pleased to be recognized. Since Dr. Agard had gone, perhaps this human might enjoy being Zeno's servant?

"Can we take him home?" the girl said.

"Oh, no," the woman said quickly.

"Why not? He looks lonely," the girl said.

Zeno blinked. "Lonely" wasn't one of his one 127 words. He had no idea what it meant. He knew he preferred to be described as brilliant and beautiful.

"Polly want a cracker?" the girl said.

"Pfft," muttered Zeno. Why did humans always ask him about Polly? Who was Polly? Why on earth would Polly want crackers? The one Zeno tried had crumbled into tasteless powder with his first chomp.

"I'm sure he's someone's pet," the woman said.

"Pet?" Zeno squawked. Dr. Agard always scolded anyone who called Zeno a pet.

"He talked, Mommy, did you hear him say 'pet'?" the girl said. "Can we keep him?"

"No, dear, he didn't really talk. He just imitated what I said. He's a bird. He has no idea what words actually mean," the woman said.

"Brawwk!" Zeno flapped his wings vigorously. No idea? How dare the woman say that. He knew what words meant. He knew plenty of things. He was confident he knew much more than the woman. Even if he didn't exactly know where to find banana-nut muffins, she probably didn't, either.

"He can't really think for himself," the woman said.

"Better to trip with the feet than with the tongue." Zeno repeated one of the human Zeno's sayings. Dr. Agard often used that quote to scold his assistant for speaking foolishly.

"Did you hear that?" the girl said.

"That just proves my point. His owner taught him those words. A parrot couldn't possibly know what they mean," the woman said.

Of course Zeno knew. Sort of. Even if he couldn't explain it. Well, he knew that the quote always made the assistant shut up for a while.

"What *does* it mean?" the girl said.

"It means we better hurry or we'll be late for your violin lesson," the woman said.

She took the girl's hand—the one without the purple circle. Together they ran down the street.

As soon as the humans had gone, Zeno thought of what he *should* have said to them.

"Zeno not pet!" he squawked.

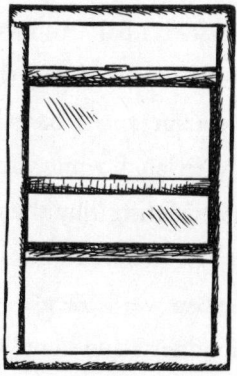

Zeno flew way up over one of Brooklyn's brownstone houses. From a window on the third floor of that house, a girl named Alya watched something gray streak across the sky. She was too far away to hear Zeno squawk. Was that a bird? she wondered. No, probably just another jet.

Her mother came in the room. Mrs. Logan straightened Alya's pillow and tucked the blankets tightly between the mattress and the railing that surrounded the bed. The bed could move in mysterious ways. Up and down and jiggling inside. Alya didn't like it. Not at all. She had said over and over again, she didn't need a hospital bed, she didn't want a hospital bed, she wasn't in a hospital. But Mrs. Logan said Alya couldn't sleep in the hammock anymore. When the bed came and filled the room, she had to lie down on it. There was no place else for her to be.

It's a shame you have to meet Alya now. You'd never guess how clever she used to be at climbing trees. Or inventing new games with a soccer ball. And you can't know what her real laugh sounded like. The one that exploded from her belly—not the whispery "ha ha" that barely tiptoed past her lips. It's hard to laugh while you're lying in bed.

You're probably wondering why she didn't get up. Alya wondered that, too. Why had her body betrayed her?

The official diagnosis was leukemia. A few months ago, doctors had done blood tests and found traitorous cells that only pretended to be the kind that fought infections. Those cells got in the way and kept Alya's real blood cells from doing their jobs. The doctors had used chemotherapy to kill the cancer cells. A fierce battle had been fought inside Alya. Unfortunately many useful cells had been destroyed, too— including the roots for Alya's dark cloud of curls. Those treatments had ended. Her hair was even starting to grow back. But for some reason her muscles still didn't want to do hardly anything anymore.

"There now," Mrs. Logan said in her most cheerful voice.

Mrs. Logan stroked Alya's head for the 9,578th time. "Your hair's growing back so soft. Just like when you were a baby."

"I'm not a baby," Alya said, and then bit her lip because she knew she sounded very much like one.

A distant bell rang.

"Someone's at the door. I bet it's Liza and Kiki." Mrs. Logan ran down the stairs.

Alya was stuck in her bed. Too late, she remembered that the plaid cap she wore for visitors was a million miles away on top of her dresser, next to the gray corner.

The corner really was the color of gloom. Her bedroom walls had been pale yellow ever since her parents hadn't known if she would be a boy or a girl. After Alya turned ten, she started planning how to redecorate her room. It took months to decide—well, Alya was busy. First there was soccer season. Then her friend Liza thought they should all be in the school play. Then Kiki signed them up for the swim team. Then they all went to sleepaway camp. In the fall, when the Logans vacationed in Puerto Rico, Alya discovered what she wanted—blue sky, crashing waves, tropical flowers, palm trees, and a real rope hammock to sleep in. She finished the waves and most of the sky before running out of blue paint. Then Alya's body had betrayed her and no one had time to even think about getting any more.

She heard her mom's voice from far away. "Come in, come in. It's so nice of you to come. Alya will be so happy to see you."

Alya thought how good at lying her mom had gotten. Of course, practice made perfect. Mrs. Logan never told the whole truth anymore. Every day she said stuff like how great Alya was doing and how cute Alya looked in a cap.

"We forgot to bring Alya's homework," Kiki said.

"I'd like to forget mine." Liza giggled.

"I'm sure she won't mind," Mrs. Logan said.

They all laughed.

"We did bring her a book," Kiki said.

"That's wonderful. Well, go on up. You know the way," Mrs. Logan said.

The girls did. They had been running up and down these steps for almost as many years as Alya herself had. Only this time her friends' footsteps told Alya what their words hadn't said. One set marched straight up. A soldier doing her duty. Sturdy sneakers. That would be Kiki. The other pair of feet scuffled along. One step forward and two steps back. Liza in her ballerina flats.

"Come on," Kiki said.

"I got something in my shoe," Liza said.

They paused at the second floor—where Alya's parents' bedroom was and the little office for her dad.

Alya wondered if she had time to get the cap. She put her hands on the railing and tried to pull herself toward the end of the bed. Her muscles quivered. She seemed to feel a thousand tiny ropes inside her arms break one at a time. She lied back down on the bed. She shut her eyes. It would be so much better if she didn't have to *see* them see her being bald. Of course they knew she had lost her hair. The cap didn't cover all the places where her curls used to be. But when she wore the cap, at least they could all pretend that everything was normal.

"Stop stalling," Kiki said.

"I'm not. I know there's a stone in there. I just can't find it."

"Let me have the shoe."

Bang bang bang. Kiki must have hit the shoe against the railing. The sound stopped and the footsteps started again.

And stopped.

"Now what?" Kiki said.

Whispering.

Kiki whispered back. Only her whispering was never as quiet as Liza's. "You don't have to plan what you're going to say. You never did before."

No, Liza never did before. However, things change. As Alya knew perfectly well.

So she planned what she was going to say. She planned how she was going to tell them that they didn't have to visit her ever again.